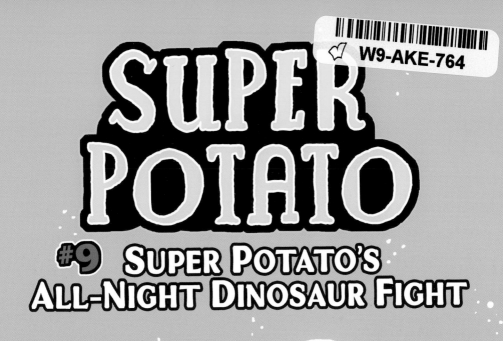

SUPER POTATO

#9 SUPER POTATO'S ALL-NIGHT DINOSAUR FIGHT

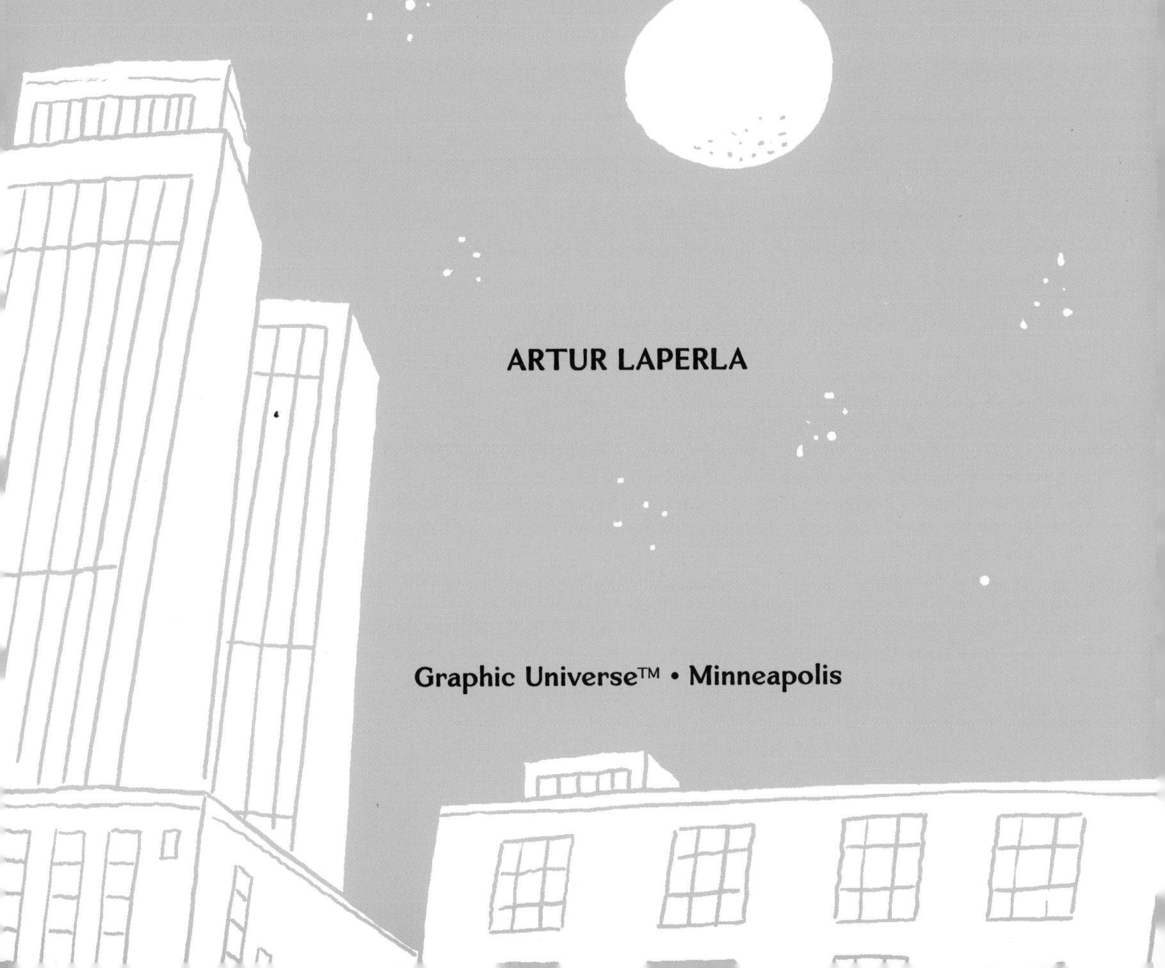

ARTUR LAPERLA

Graphic Universe™ • Minneapolis

Story and illustrations by Artur Laperla
Translation by Norwyn MacTíre

First American edition published in 2022 by Graphic Universe™

Copyright © 2020 by Artur Laperla and Bang. Ediciones. Published by arrangement with S.B.Rights Agency.

Graphic Universe™ is a trademark of Lerner Publishing Group, Inc.

Graphic Universe™
An imprint of Lerner Publishing Group, Inc.
241 First Avenue North
Minneapolis, MN 55401 USA

For reading levels and more information, look up this title at www.lernerbooks.com.

Main body text set in CCWildWords. Typeface provided by Comicraft.

Library of Congress Cataloging-in-Publication Data

Names: Laperla (Artist), author, illustrator.
Title: Super Potato's all-night dinosaur fight / Artur Laperla.
Other titles: Super Patata (Series). English
Description: First American edition. | Minneapolis : Graphic Universe, 2022. | Series: Super Potato ; book 9 | Audience: Ages 7–11 | Audience: Grades 2–3 | Summary: "When Malicia the Malignant sends dozens of dinosaurs to fight Super Potato, the number of prehistoric pests keeps him awake for days. How do you defeat a T-Rex on 42 hours with no sleep?"— Provided by publisher.
Identifiers: LCCN 2021047113 (print) | LCCN 2021047114 (ebook) | ISBN 9781728424590 (library binding) | ISBN 9781728462950 (paperback) | ISBN 9781728461014 (ebook)
Subjects: CYAC: Graphic novels. | Superheroes—Fiction. | Potatoes—Fiction. | Dinosaurs—Fiction. | Humorous stories. | LCGFT: Superhero comics. | Humorous comics. | Graphic novels.
Classification: LCC PZ7.7.L367 Stn 2022 (print) | LCC PZ7.7.L367 (ebook) | DDC 741.5/973—dc23/eng/20211006

LC record available at https://lccn.loc.gov/2021047113
LC ebook record available at https://lccn.loc.gov/2021047114

Manufactured in the United States of America
1-49328-49444-12/10/2021

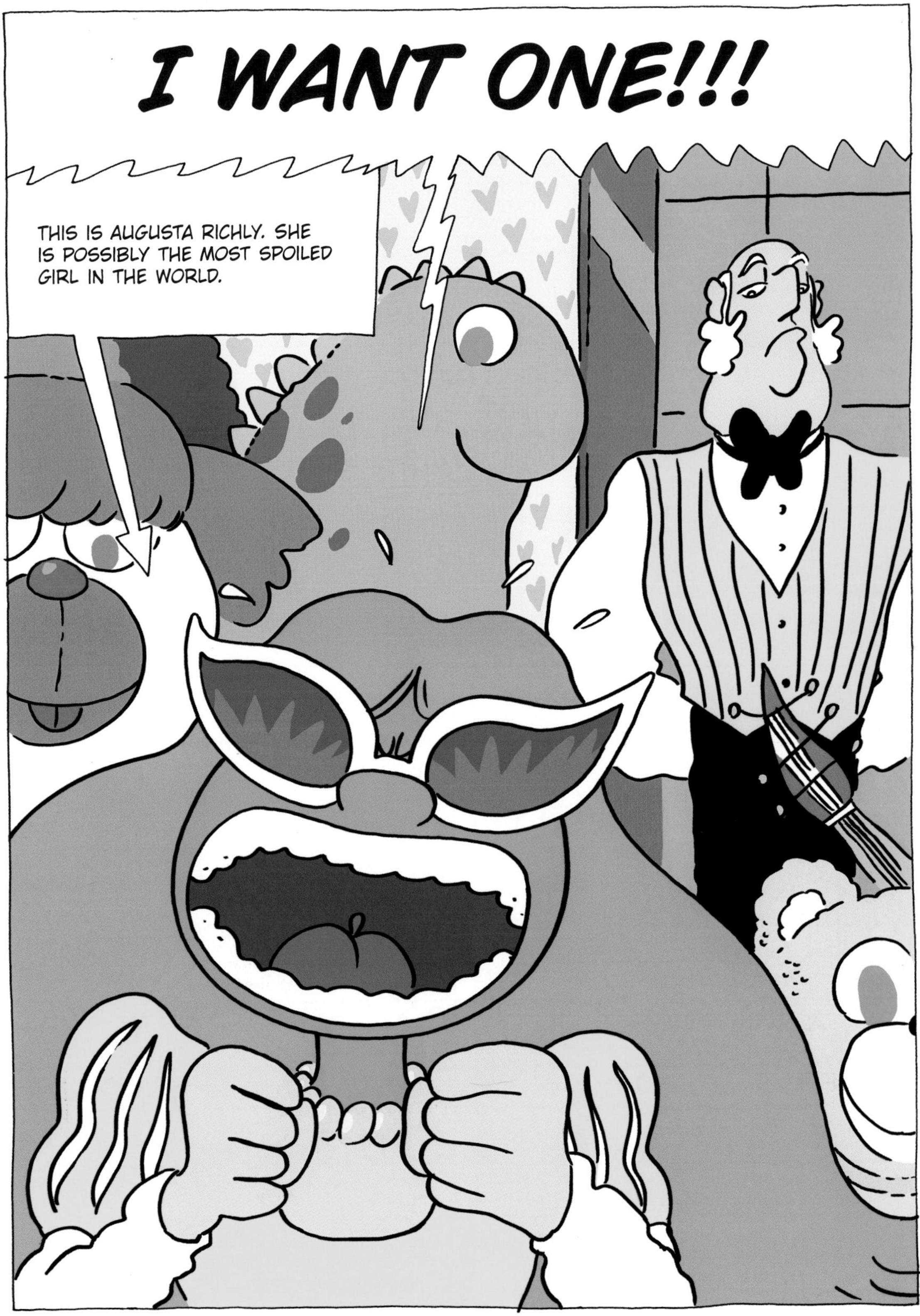
I WANT ONE!!!
THIS IS AUGUSTA RICHLY. SHE IS POSSIBLY THE MOST SPOILED GIRL IN THE WORLD.

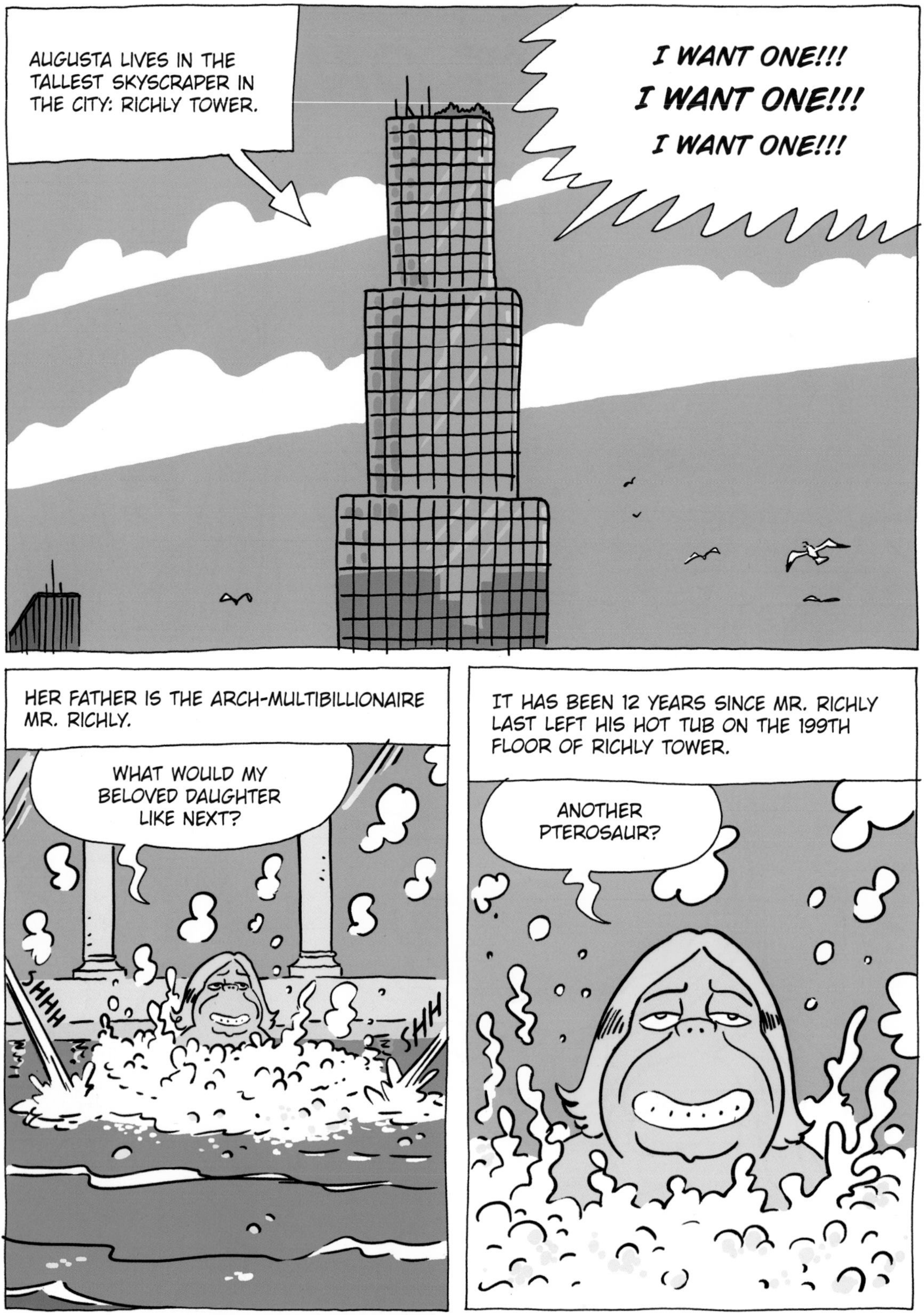
AUGUSTA LIVES IN THE TALLEST SKYSCRAPER IN THE CITY: RICHLY TOWER.
I WANT ONE!!! I WANT ONE!!! I WANT ONE!!!
HER FATHER IS THE ARCH-MULTIBILLIONAIRE MR. RICHLY.
WHAT WOULD MY BELOVED DAUGHTER LIKE NEXT?
IT HAS BEEN 12 YEARS SINCE MR. RICHLY LAST LEFT HIS HOT TUB ON THE 199TH FLOOR OF RICHLY TOWER.
ANOTHER PTEROSAUR?

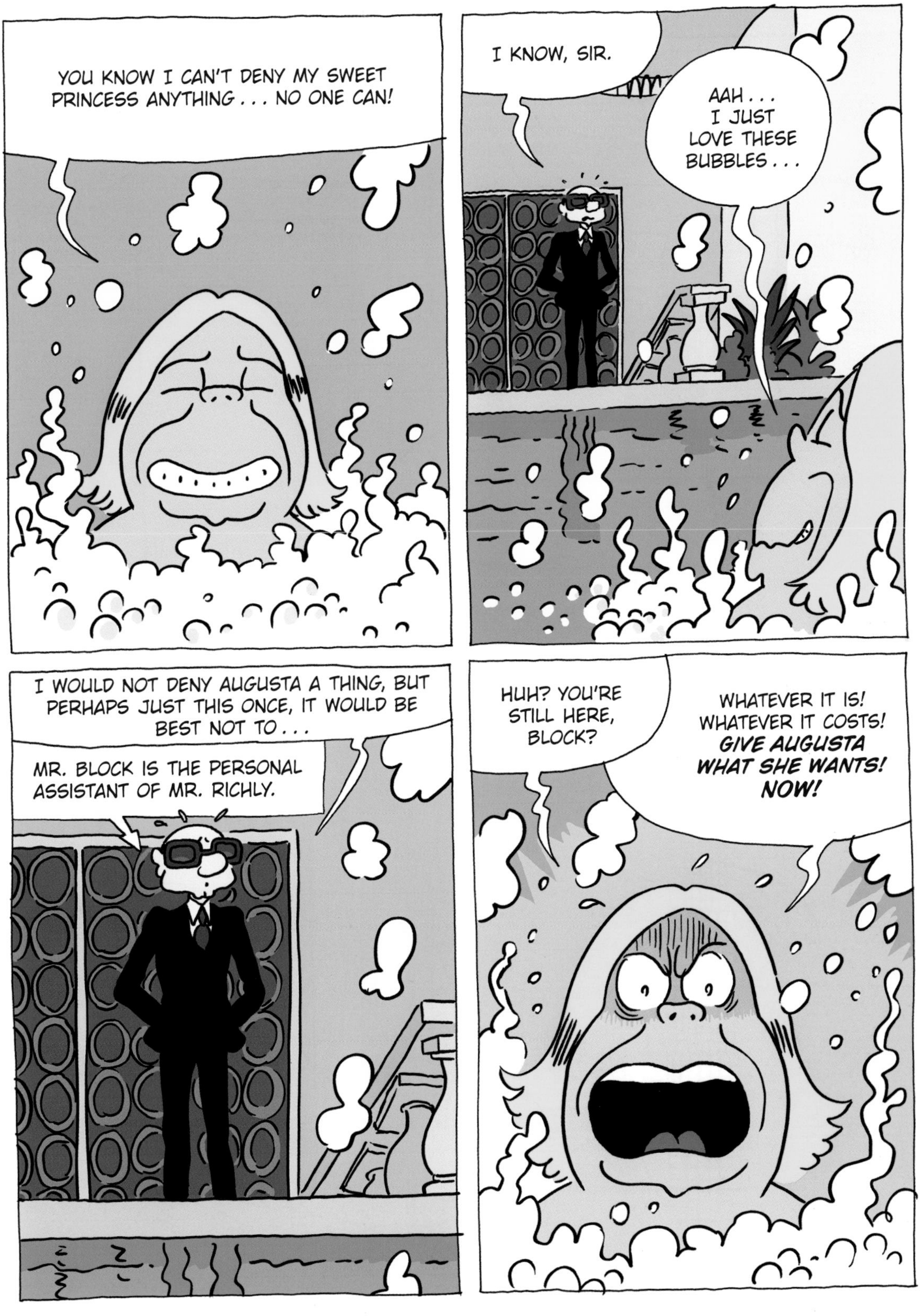
YOU KNOW I CAN'T DENY MY SWEET PRINCESS ANYTHING . . . NO ONE CAN!
I KNOW, SIR.
AAH . . . I JUST LOVE THESE BUBBLES . . .
I WOULD NOT DENY AUGUSTA A THING, BUT PERHAPS JUST THIS ONCE, IT WOULD BE BEST NOT TO . . .
MR. BLOCK IS THE PERSONAL ASSISTANT OF MR. RICHLY.
HUH? YOU'RE STILL HERE, BLOCK?
WHATEVER IT IS! WHATEVER IT COSTS! *GIVE AUGUSTA WHAT SHE WANTS! NOW!*

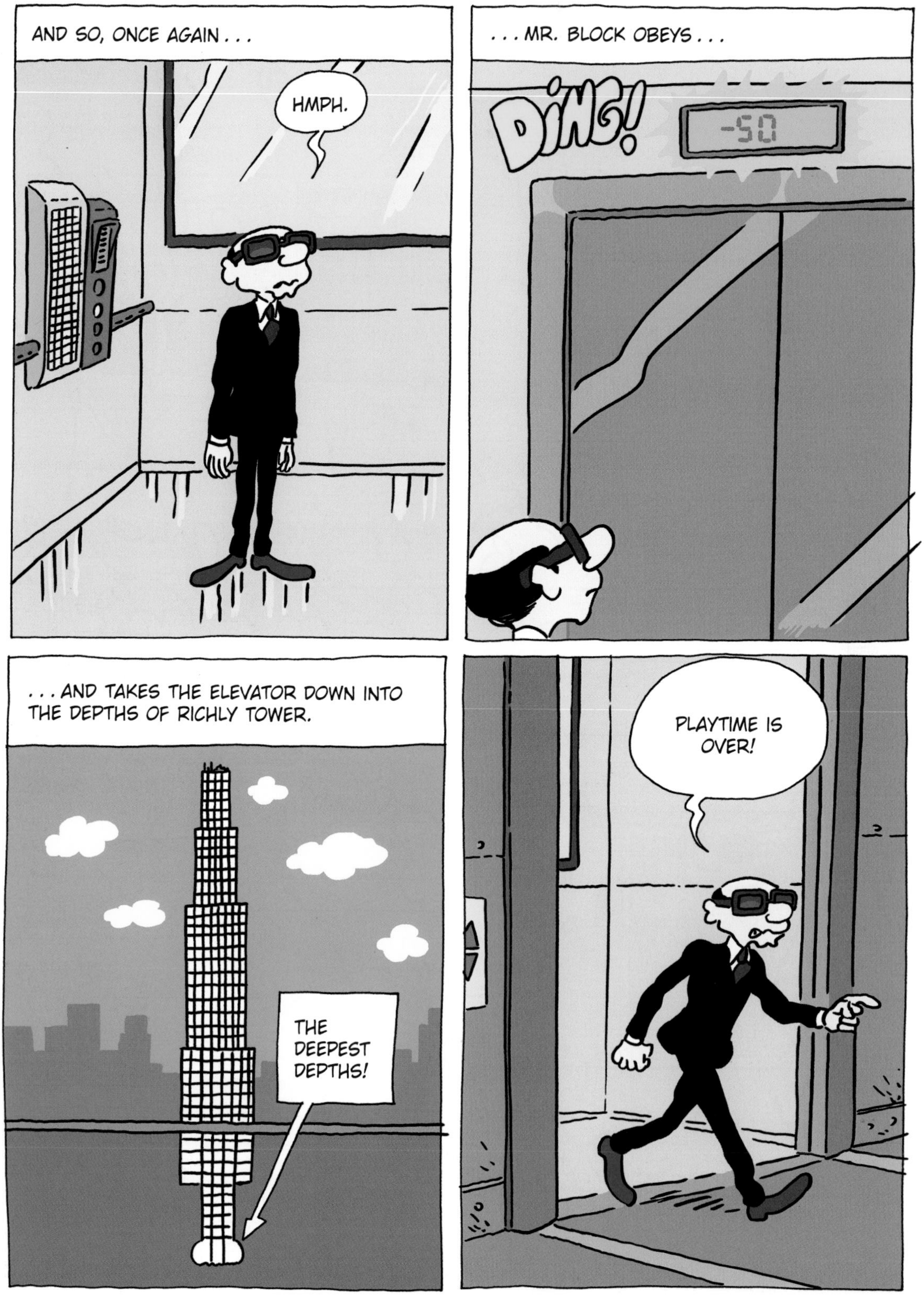

AND SO, ONCE AGAIN . . .
HMPH.
. . . MR. BLOCK OBEYS . . .
DING!
-50
. . . AND TAKES THE ELEVATOR DOWN INTO THE DEPTHS OF RICHLY TOWER.
THE DEEPEST DEPTHS!
PLAYTIME IS OVER!

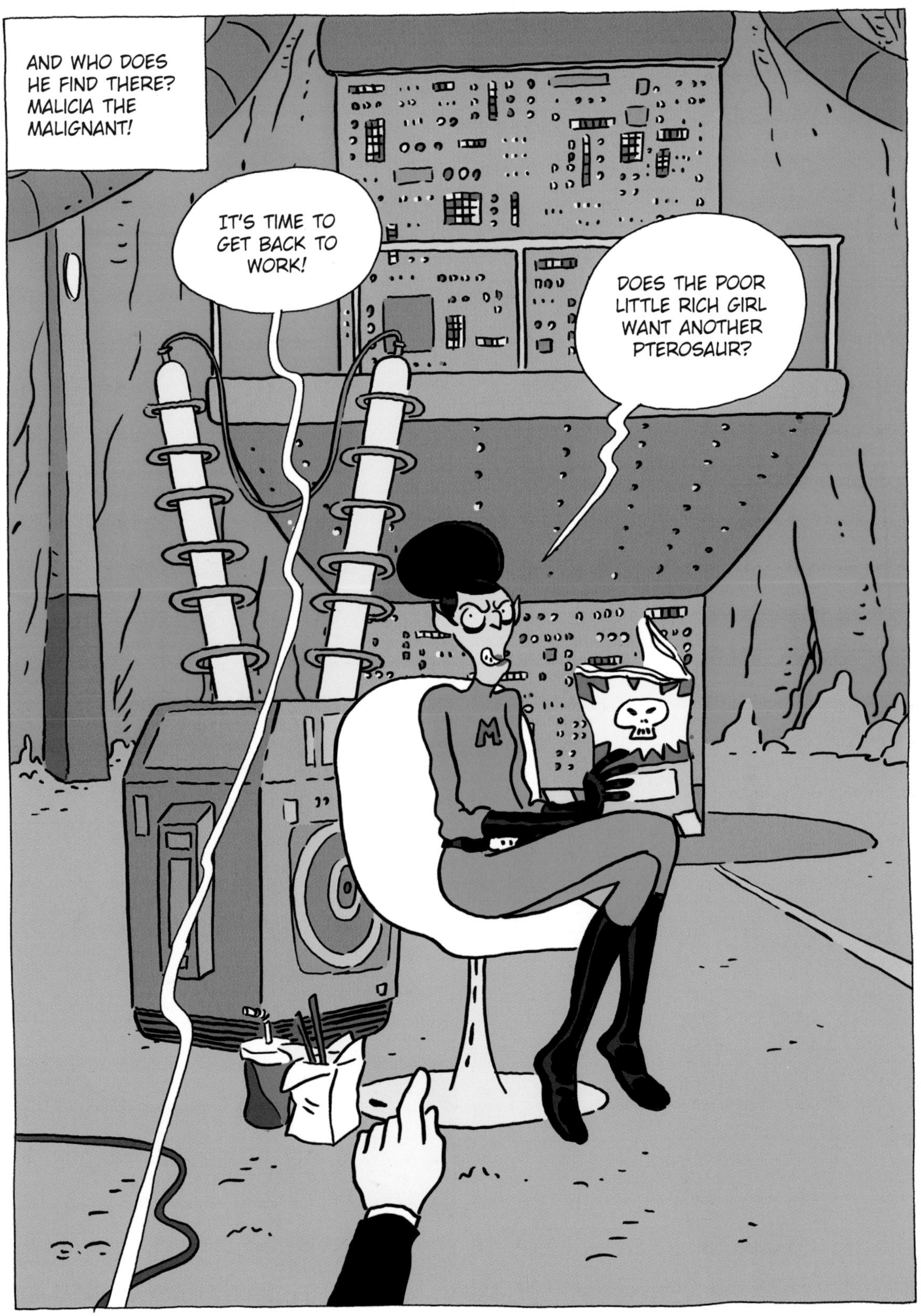
AND WHO DOES HE FIND THERE? MALICIA THE MALIGNANT!
IT'S TIME TO GET BACK TO WORK!
DOES THE POOR LITTLE RICH GIRL WANT ANOTHER PTEROSAUR?

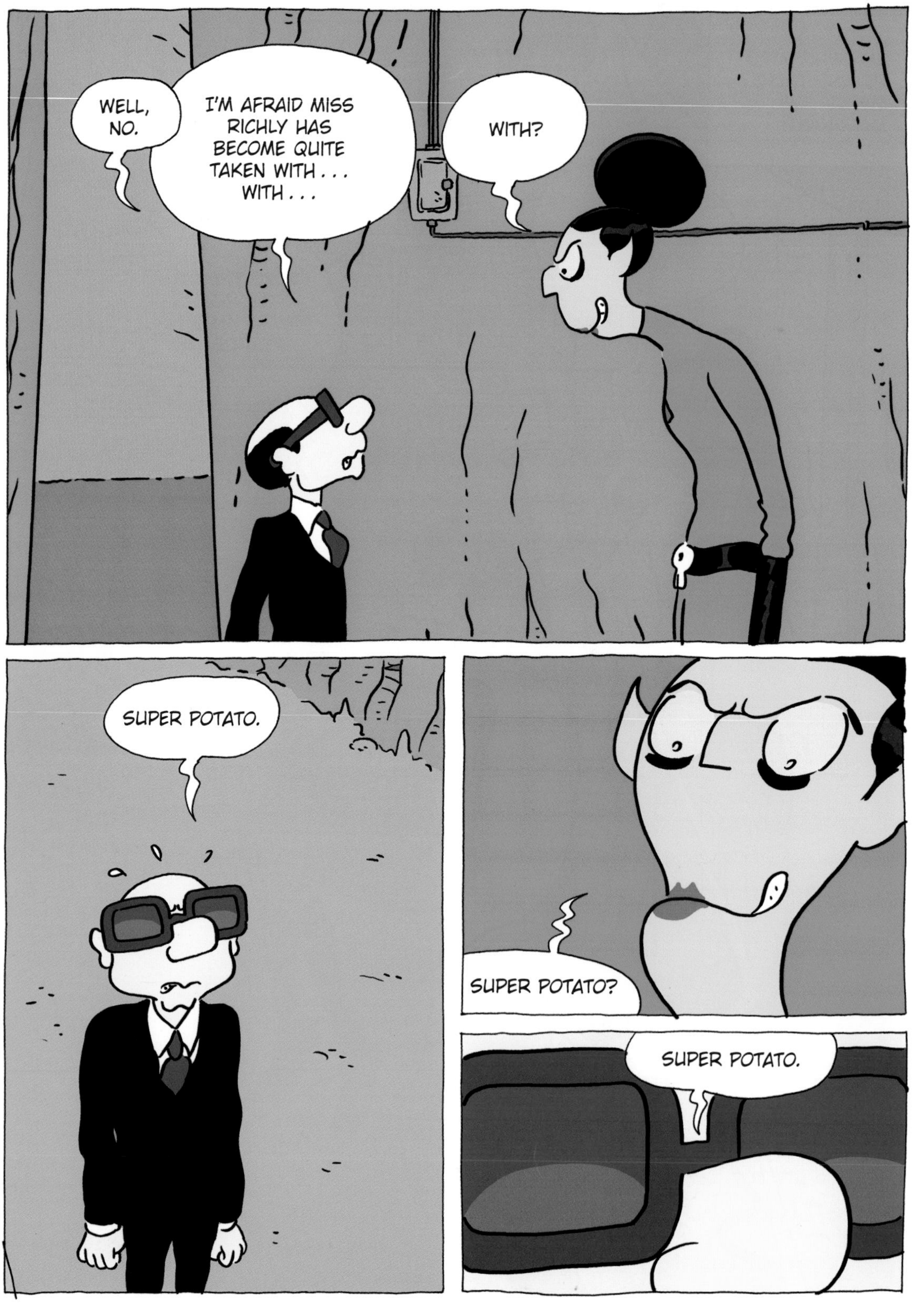
WELL, NO.
I'M AFRAID MISS RICHLY HAS BECOME QUITE TAKEN WITH . . . WITH . . .
WITH?
SUPER POTATO.
SUPER POTATO?
SUPER POTATO.

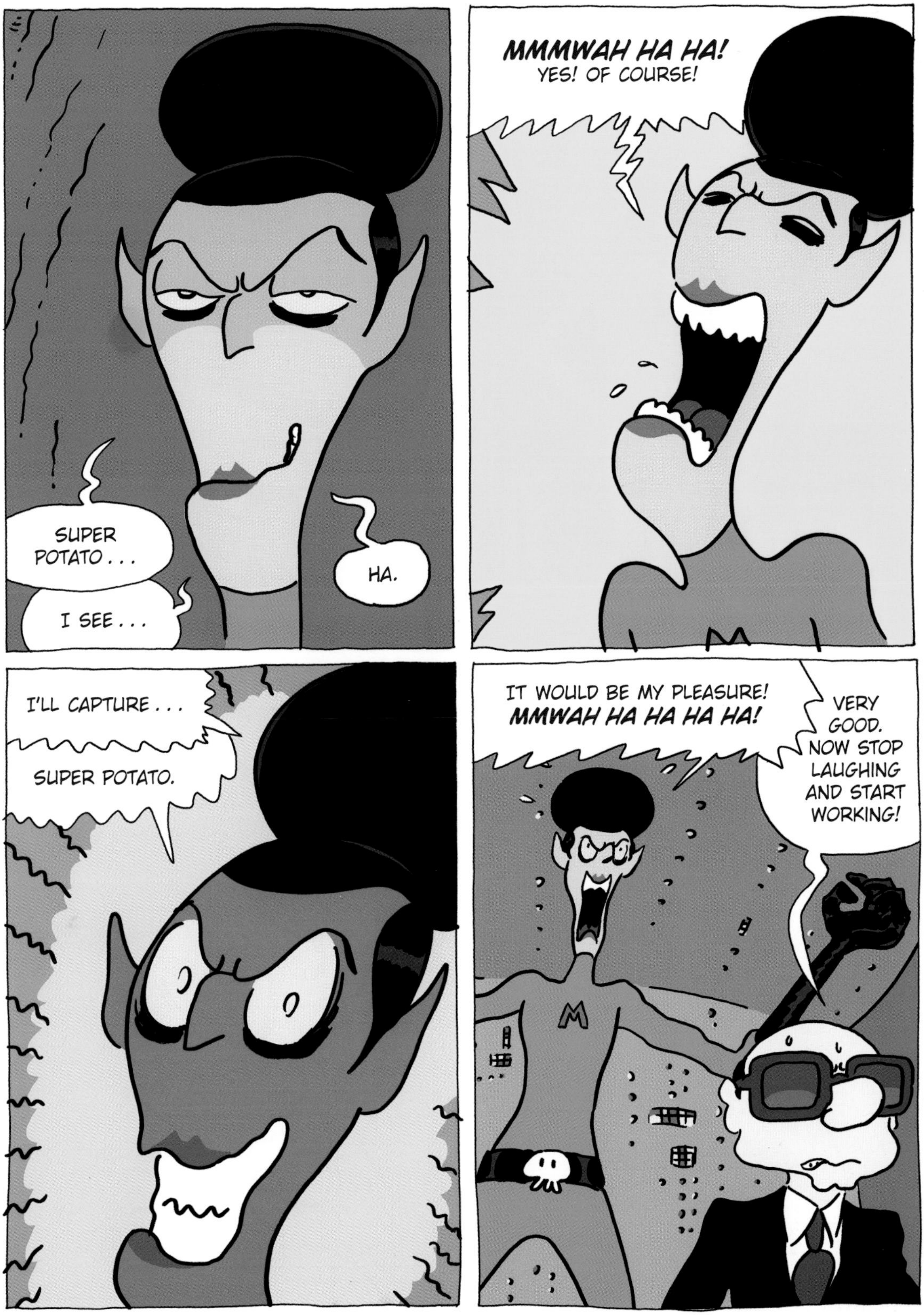
SUPER POTATO . . .
I SEE . . .
HA.
MMMWAH HA HA!
YES! OF COURSE!
I'LL CAPTURE . . .
SUPER POTATO.
IT WOULD BE MY PLEASURE!
MMWAH HA HA HA HA!
VERY GOOD. NOW STOP LAUGHING AND START WORKING!

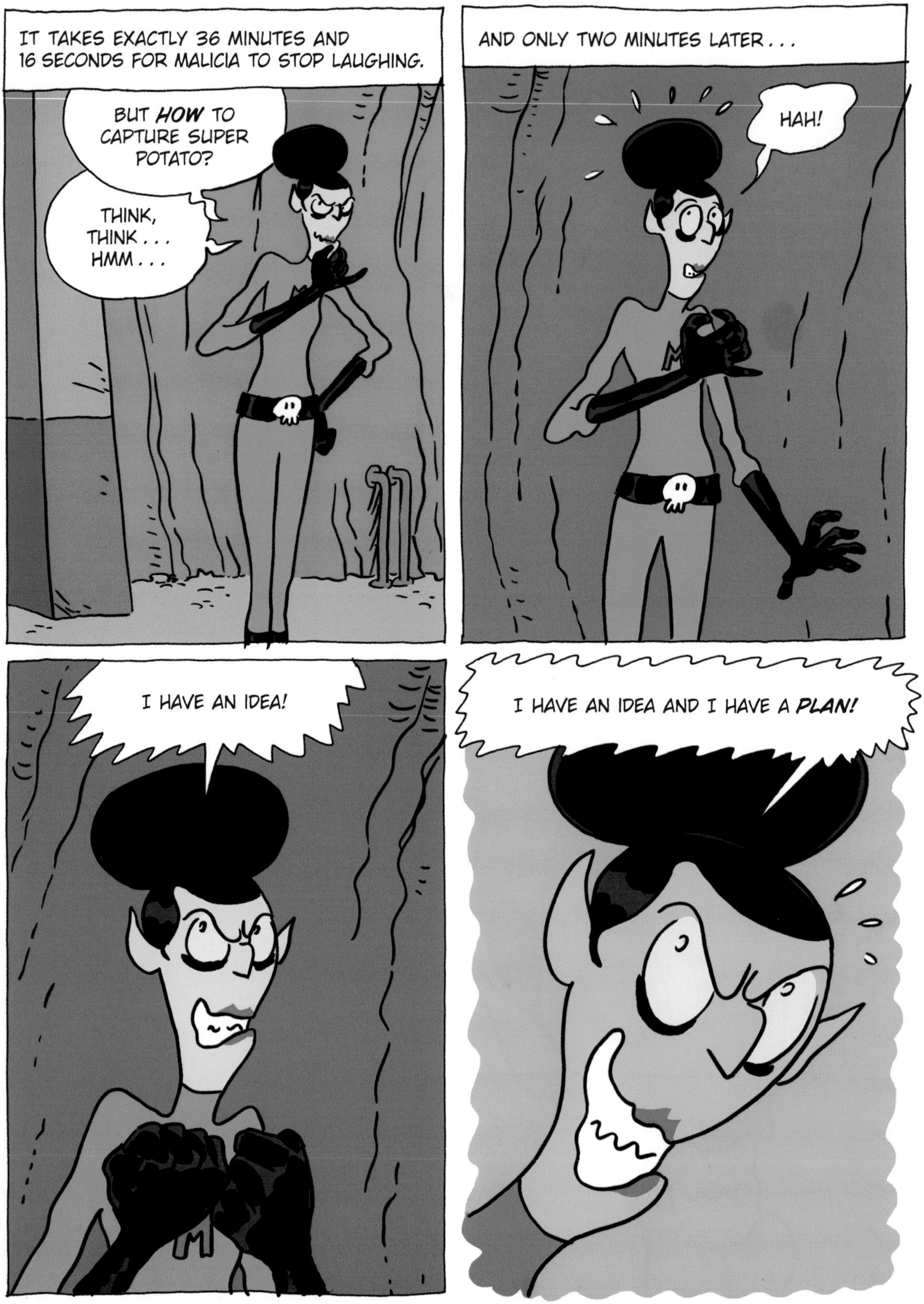
IT TAKES EXACTLY 36 MINUTES AND 16 SECONDS FOR MALICIA TO STOP LAUGHING.
BUT HOW TO CAPTURE SUPER POTATO?
THINK, THINK . . . HMM . . .
AND ONLY TWO MINUTES LATER . . .
HAH!
I HAVE AN IDEA!
I HAVE AN IDEA AND I HAVE A PLAN!

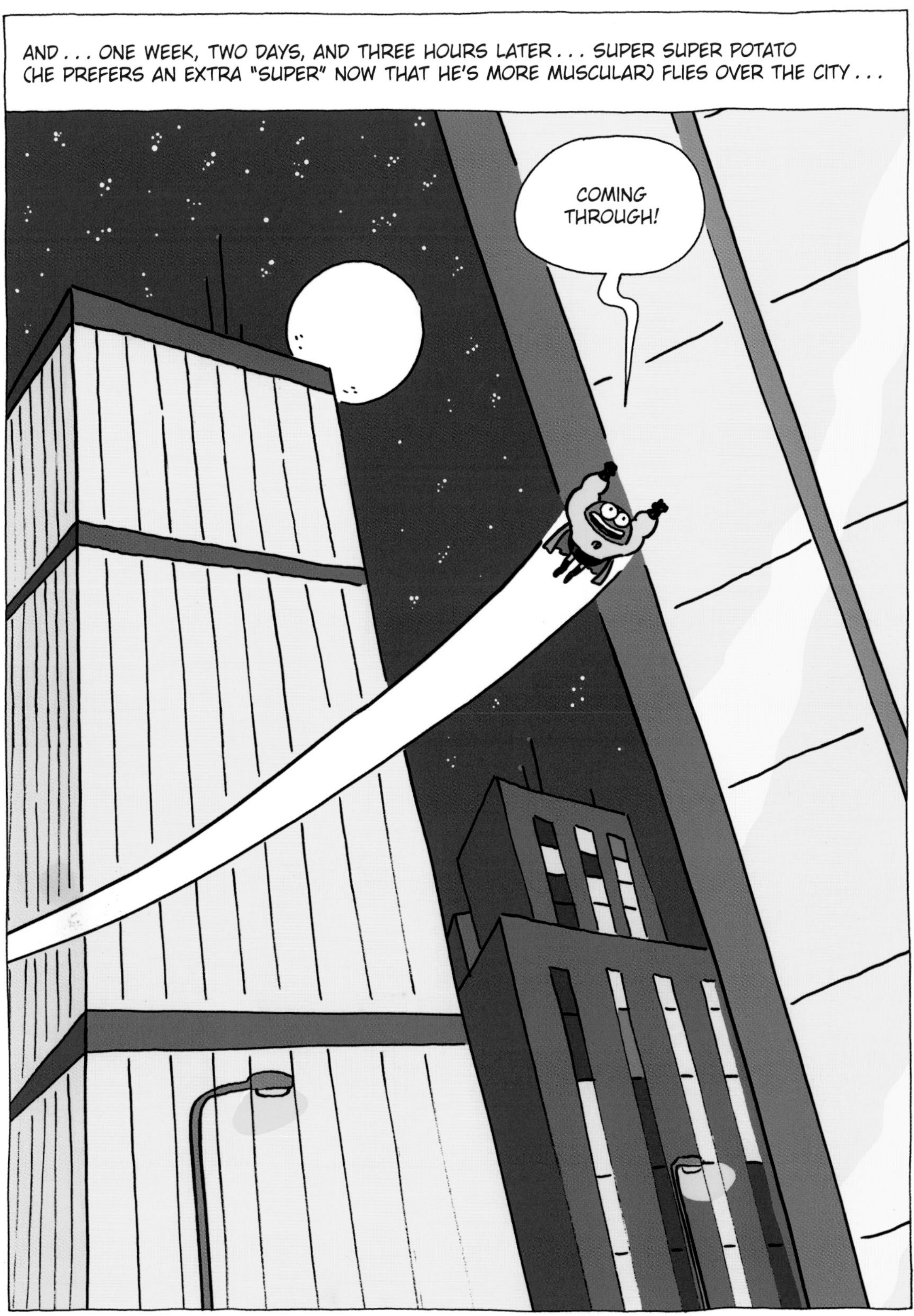
AND . . . ONE WEEK, TWO DAYS, AND THREE HOURS LATER . . . SUPER SUPER POTATO (HE PREFERS AN EXTRA "SUPER" NOW THAT HE'S MORE MUSCULAR) FLIES OVER THE CITY . . .
COMING THROUGH!

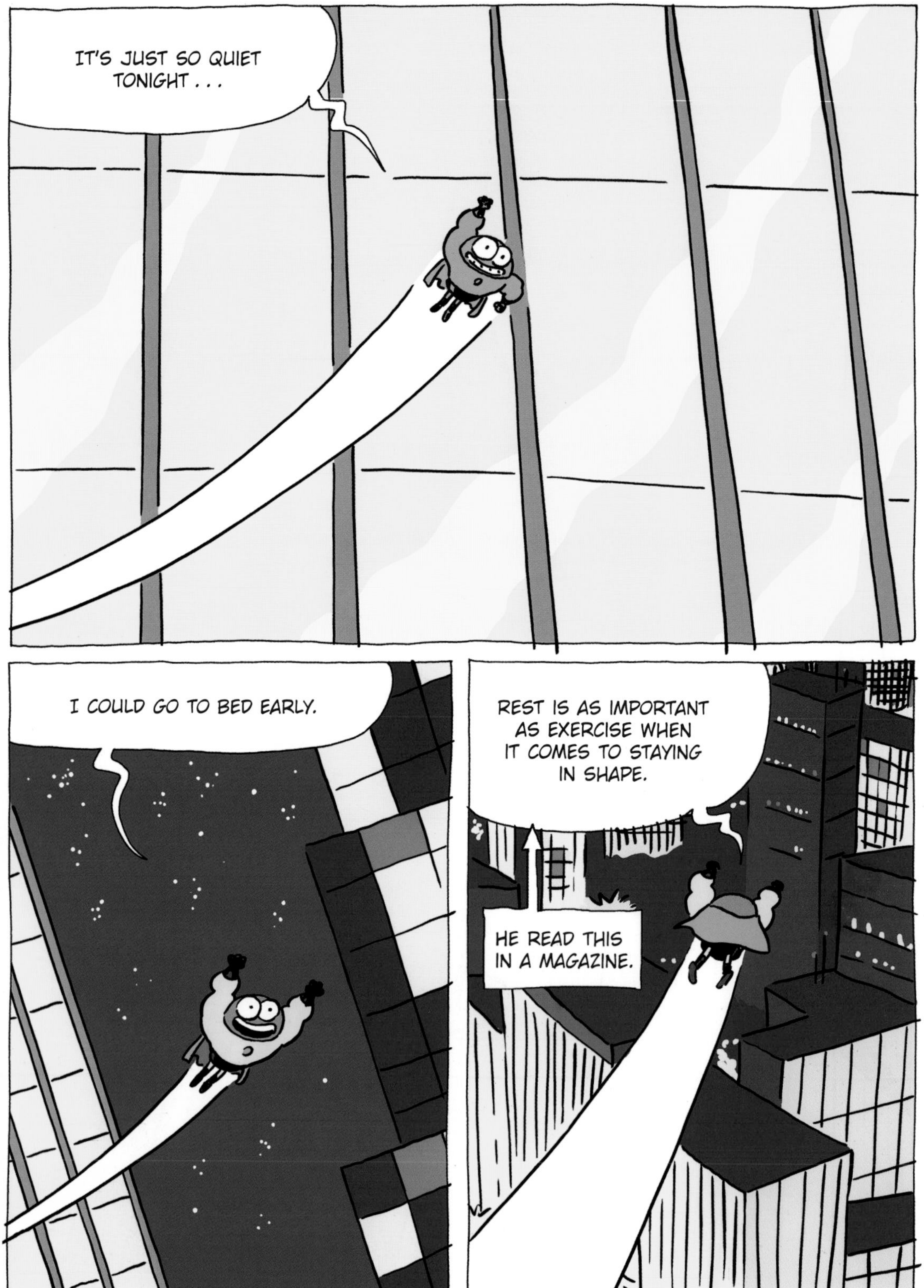
IT'S JUST SO QUIET TONIGHT . . .
I COULD GO TO BED EARLY.
REST IS AS IMPORTANT AS EXERCISE WHEN IT COMES TO STAYING IN SHAPE.
HE READ THIS IN A MAGAZINE.

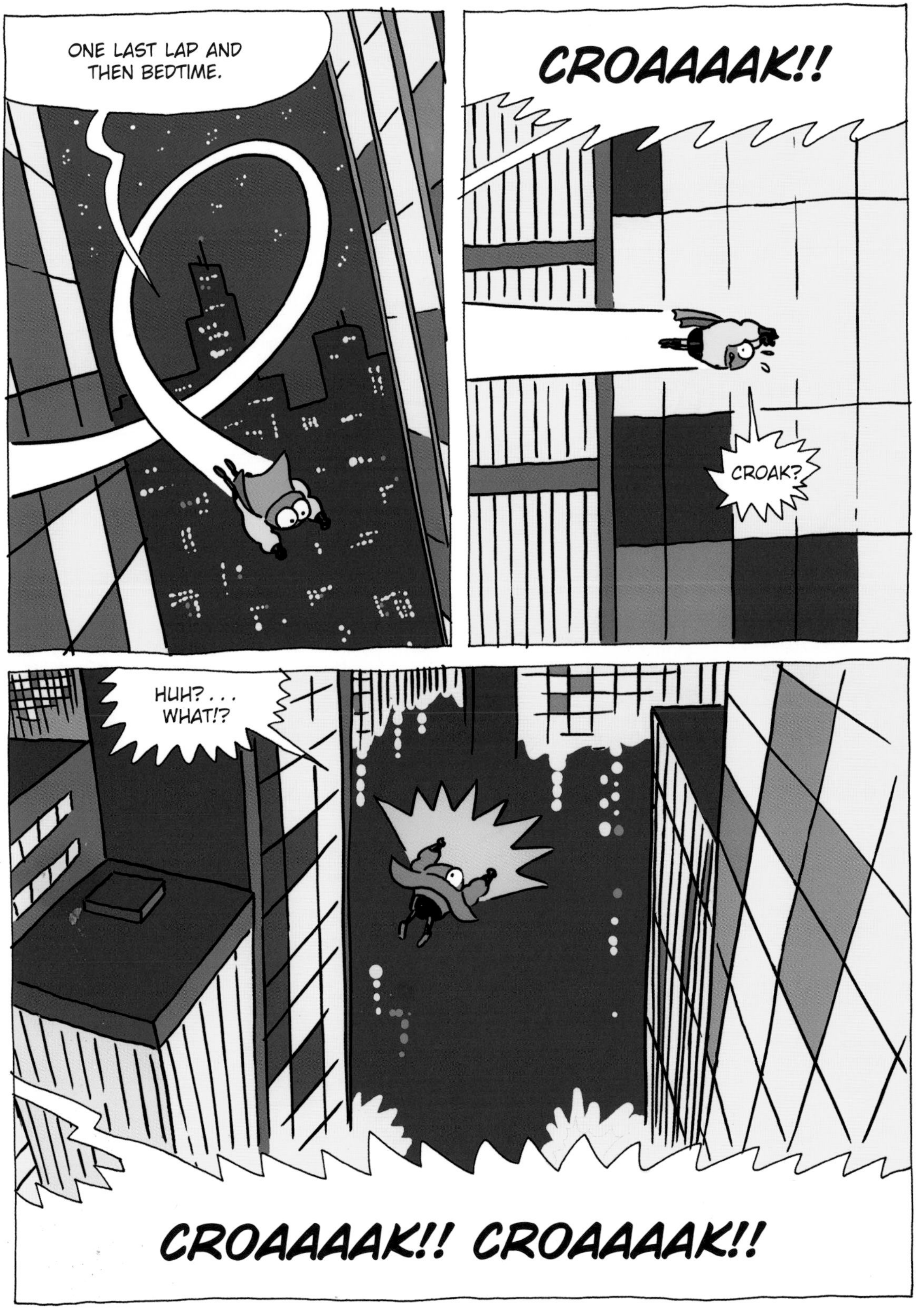
ONE LAST LAP AND THEN BEDTIME.
CROAAAAK!!
CROAK?
HUH? . . . WHAT!?
CROAAAAK!! CROAAAAK!!

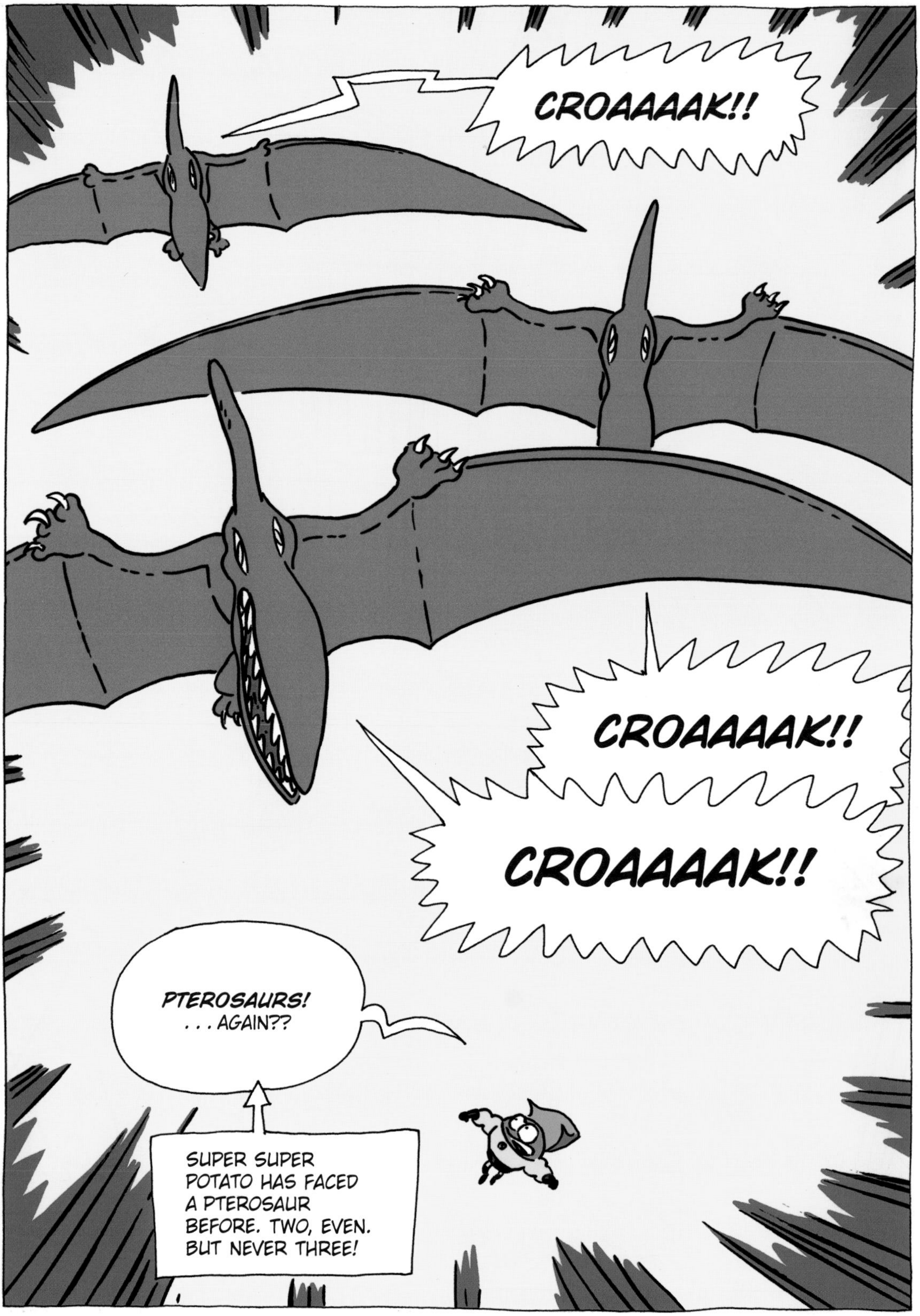
CROAAAAK!!
CROAAAAK!!
CROAAAAK!!
PTEROSAURS! . . . AGAIN??
SUPER SUPER POTATO HAS FACED A PTEROSAUR BEFORE. TWO, EVEN. BUT NEVER THREE!

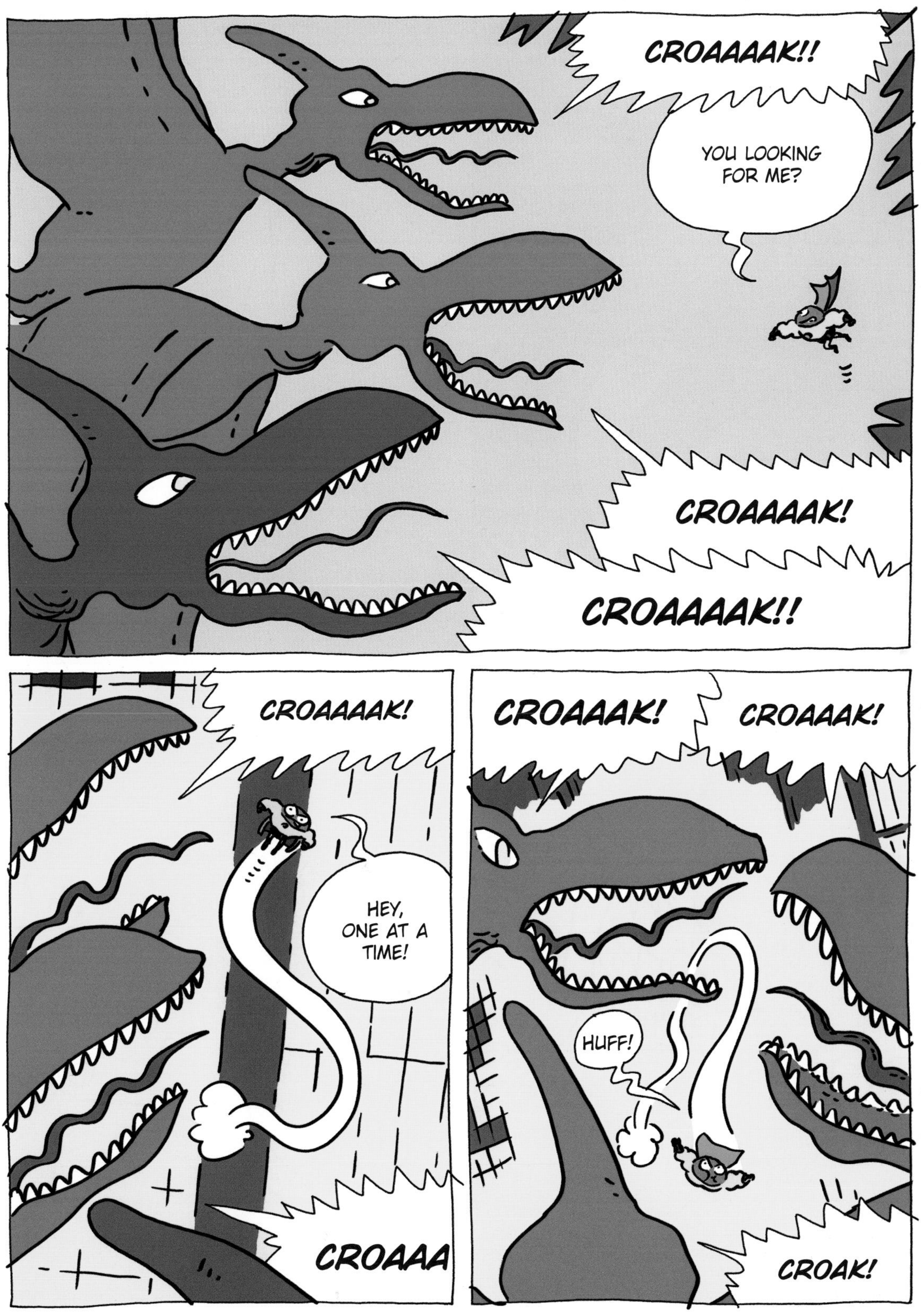
CROAAAAK!!
YOU LOOKING FOR ME?
CROAAAAK!
CROAAAAK!!
CROAAAAK!
HEY, ONE AT A TIME!
CROAAA
CROAAAK!
CROAAAK!
HUFF!
CROAK!

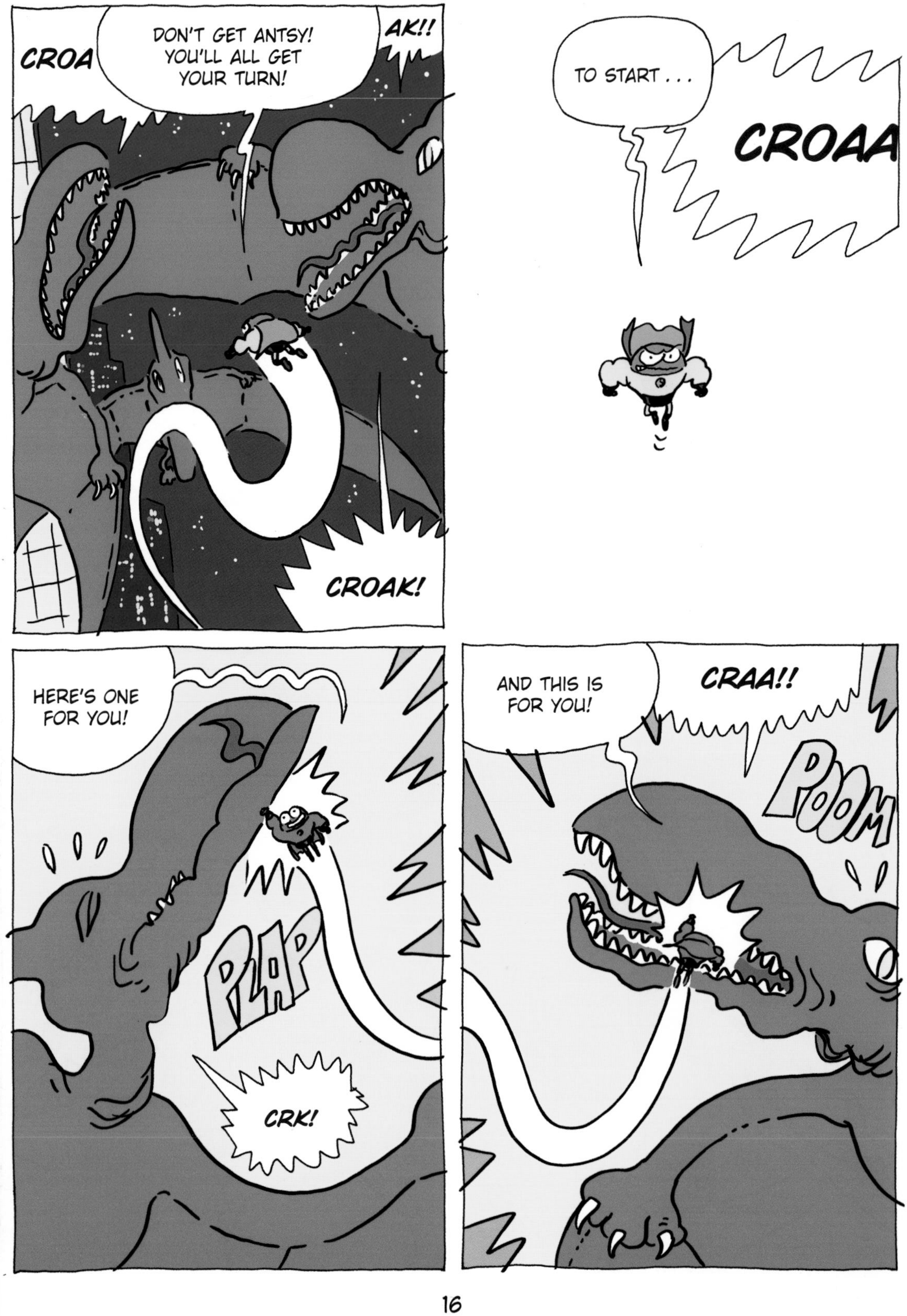
CROA
DON'T GET ANTSY! YOU'LL ALL GET YOUR TURN!
AK!!
CROAK!
TO START . . .
CROAA
HERE'S ONE FOR YOU!
PLAP
CRK!
AND THIS IS FOR YOU!
CRAA!!
POOM

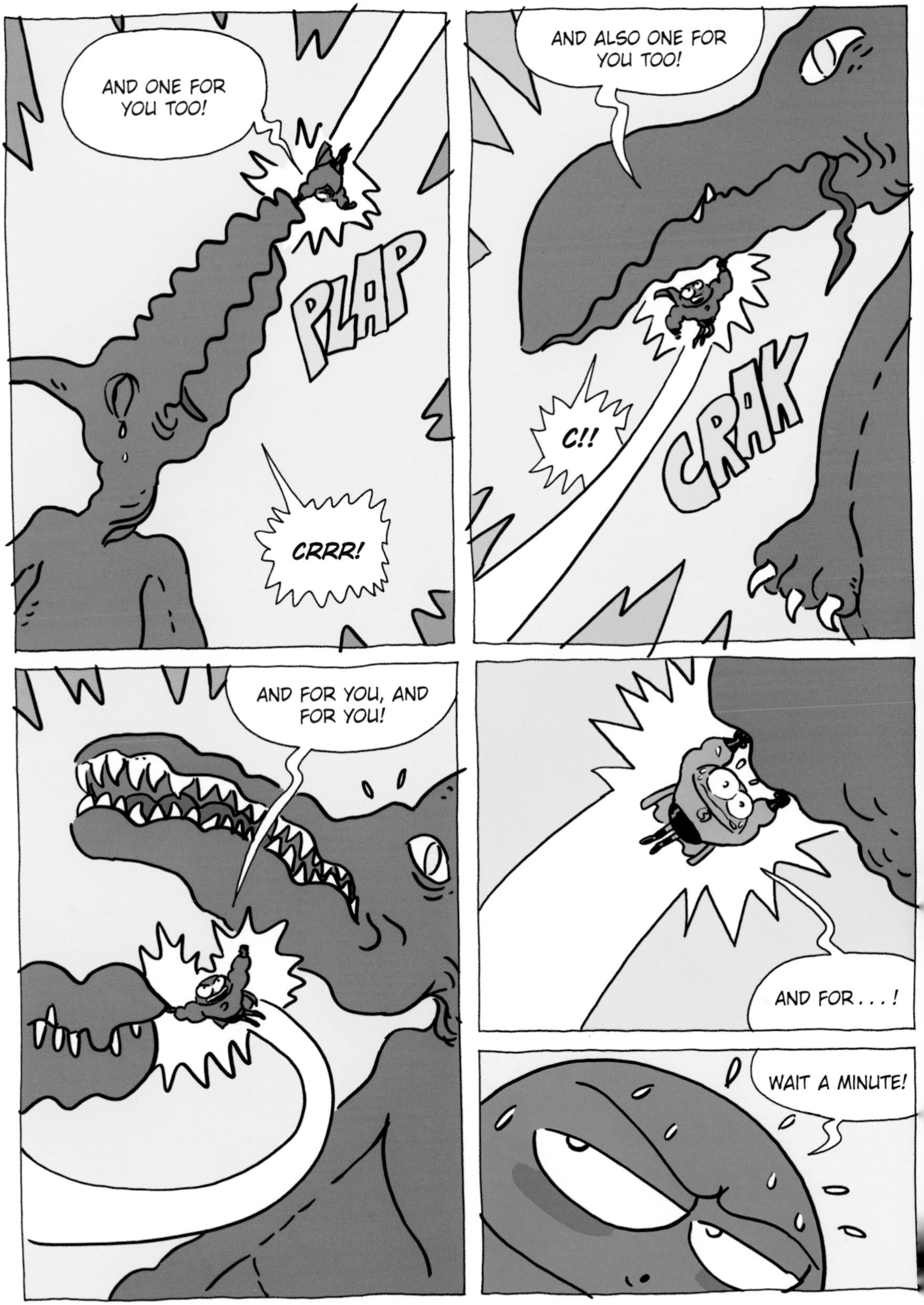
AND ONE FOR YOU TOO!
PLAP
CRRR!
AND ALSO ONE FOR YOU TOO!
C!!
CRAK
AND FOR YOU, AND FOR YOU!
AND FOR . . . !
WAIT A MINUTE!

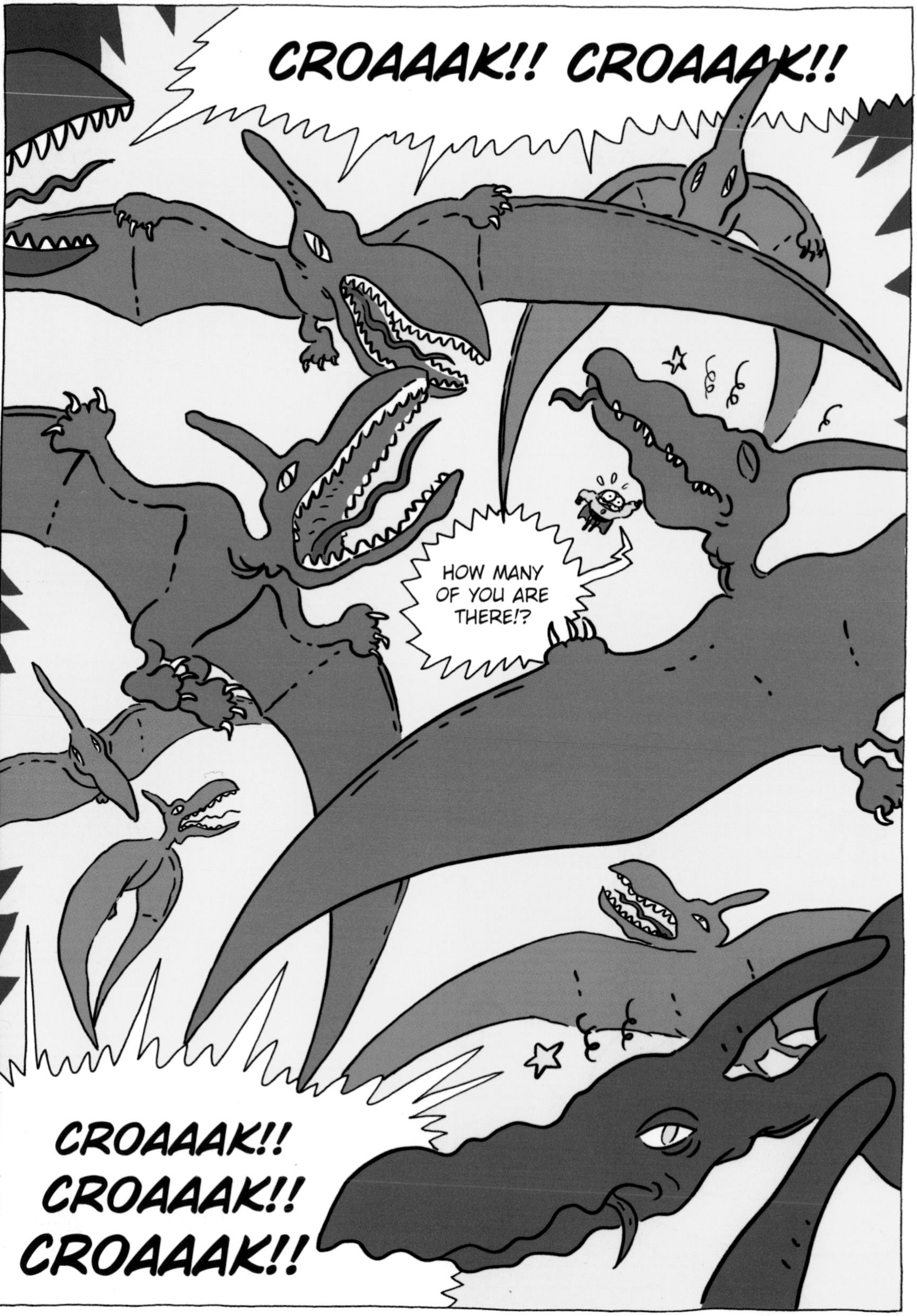
CROAAAK!! CROAAAK!!
HOW MANY OF YOU ARE THERE!?
CROAAAK!! CROAAAK!! CROAAAK!!

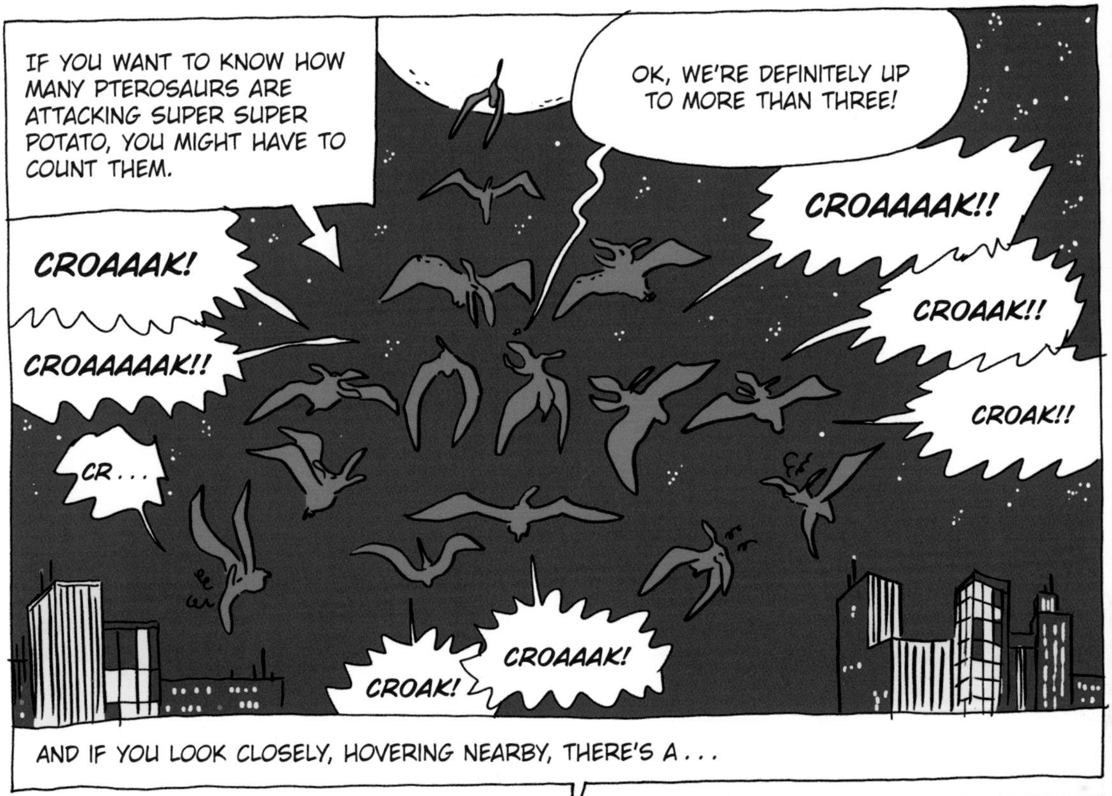
IF YOU WANT TO KNOW HOW MANY PTEROSAURS ARE ATTACKING SUPER SUPER POTATO, YOU MIGHT HAVE TO COUNT THEM.
OK, WE'RE DEFINITELY UP TO MORE THAN THREE!
CROAAAAK!!
CROAAAK!
CROAAK!!
CROAAAAAAK!!
CROAK!!
CR . . .
CROAAAK!
CROAK!
AND IF YOU LOOK CLOSELY, HOVERING NEARBY, THERE'S A . . .

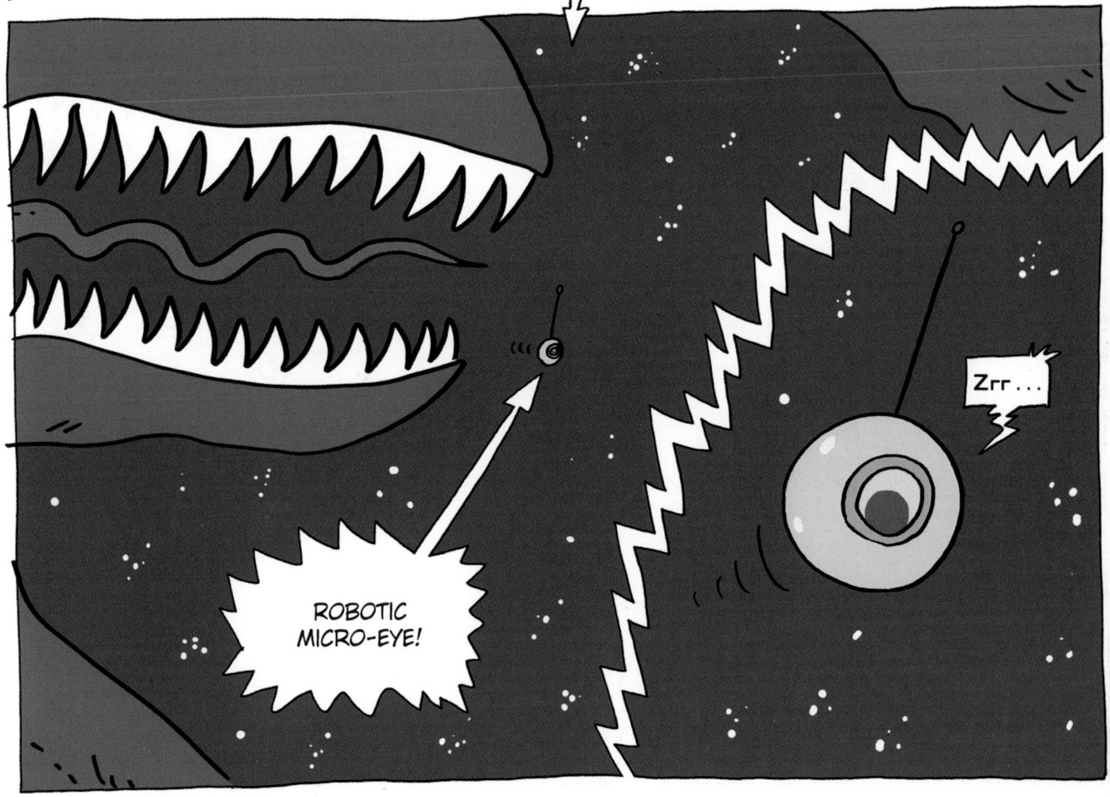
Zrr . . .
ROBOTIC MICRO-EYE!

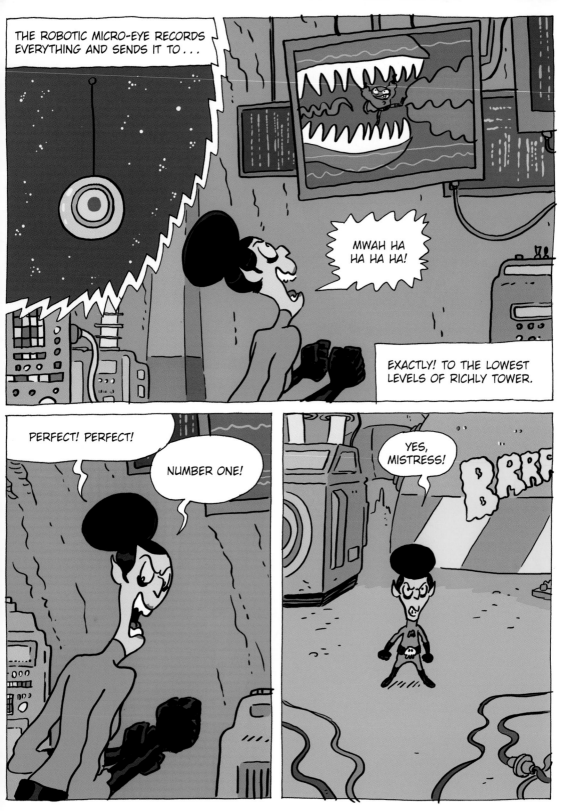

THE ROBOTIC MICRO-EYE RECORDS EVERYTHING AND SENDS IT TO...

MWAH HA HA HA HA!

EXACTLY! TO THE LOWEST LEVELS OF RICHLY TOWER.

PERFECT! PERFECT!

NUMBER ONE!

YES, MISTRESS!

BRRR

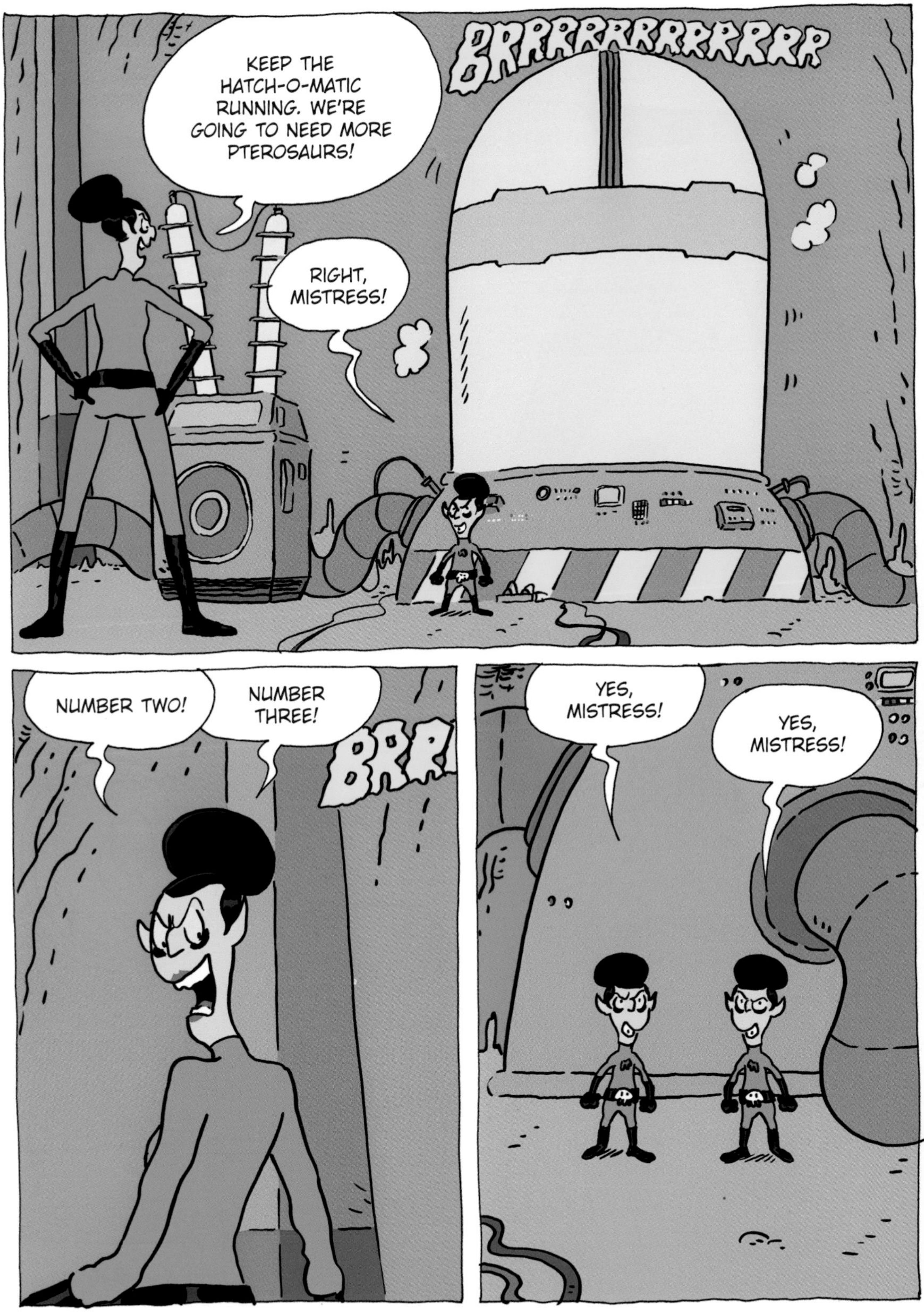
BRRRRRRRRRRRR
KEEP THE HATCH-O-MATIC RUNNING. WE'RE GOING TO NEED MORE PTEROSAURS!
RIGHT, MISTRESS!
NUMBER TWO!
NUMBER THREE!
BRR
YES, MISTRESS!
YES, MISTRESS!

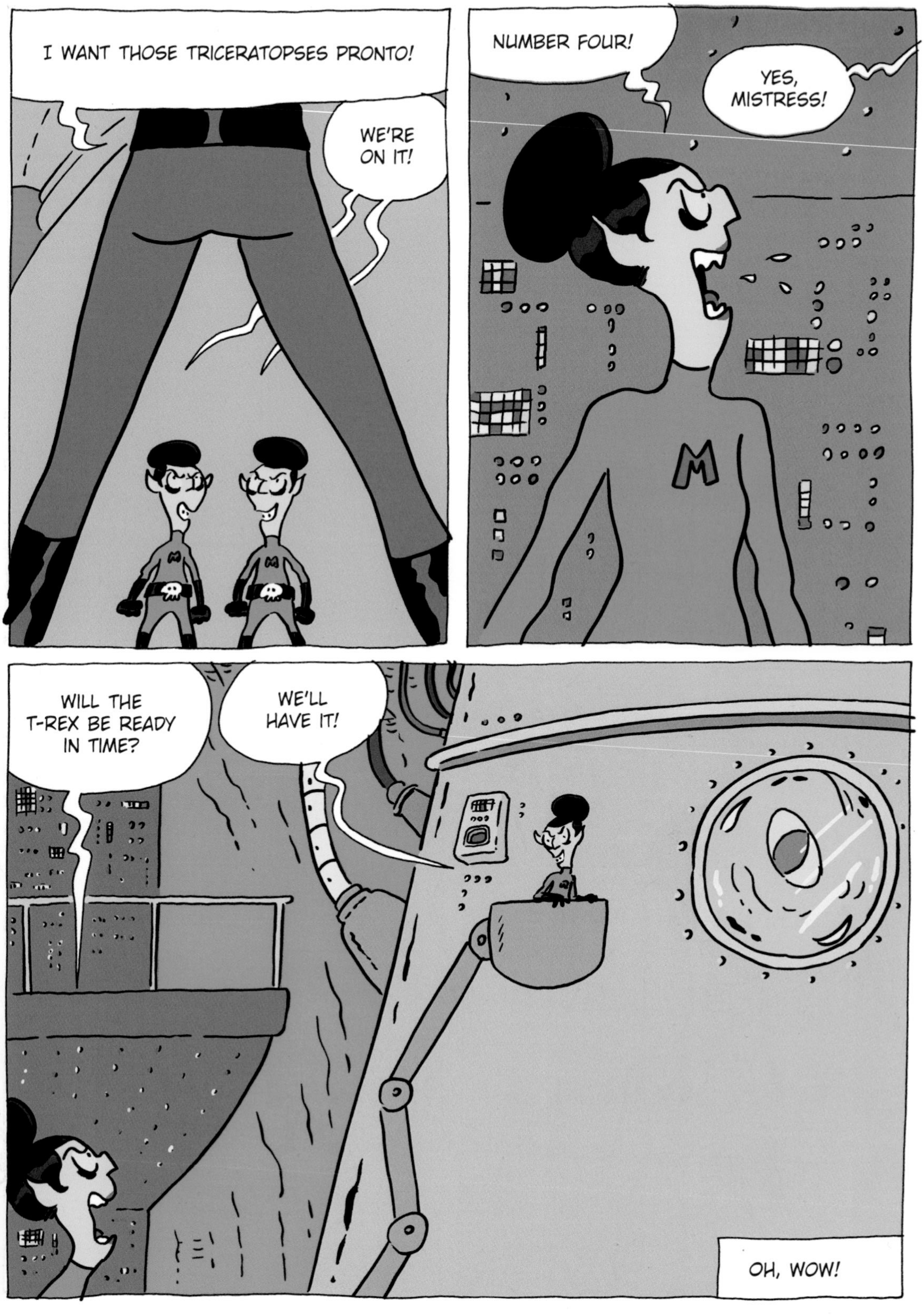
I WANT THOSE TRICERATOPSES PRONTO!
WE'RE ON IT!
NUMBER FOUR!
YES, MISTRESS!
WILL THE T-REX BE READY IN TIME?
WE'LL HAVE IT!
OH, WOW!

MALICIA'S PLAN TO CAPTURE SUPER SUPER POTATO IS UNDERWAY! AND IT'S CLEAR THE PLAN INCLUDES: FOUR MINI-CLONES, A WHOLE HEAP OF PTEROSAURS, WHO KNOWS HOW MANY TRICERATOPSES, AND LAST BUT NOT LEAST, A T-REX.

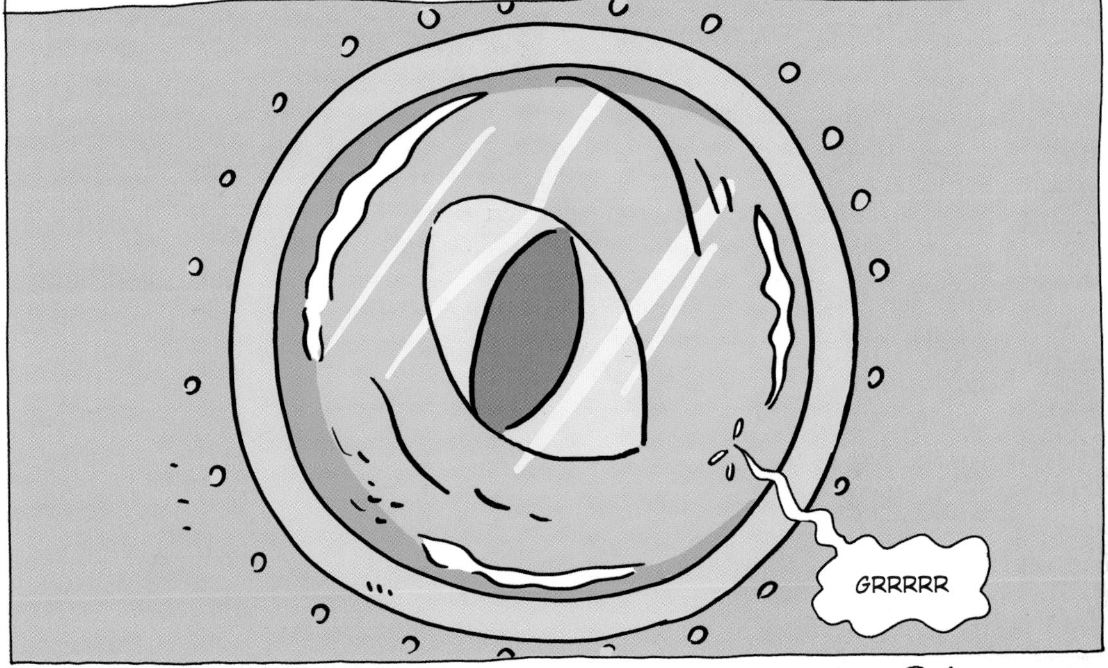
GRRRRR

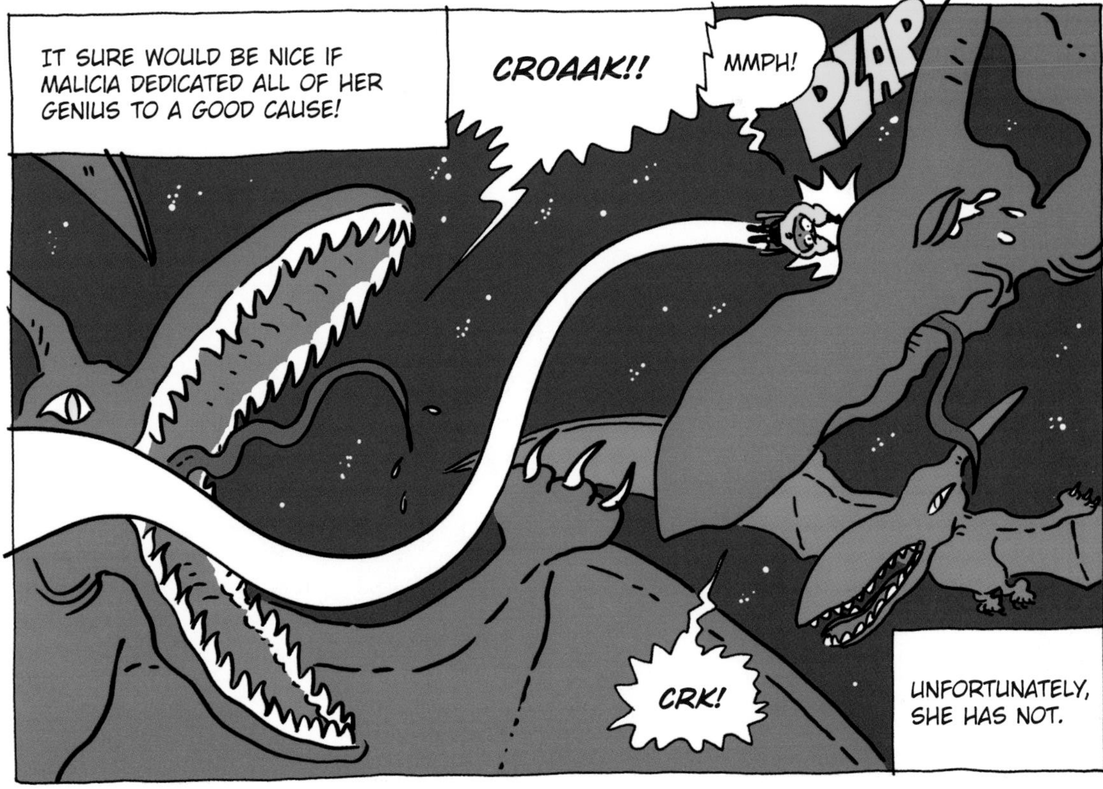
IT SURE WOULD BE NICE IF MALICIA DEDICATED ALL OF HER GENIUS TO A GOOD CAUSE!
CROAAK!!
MMPH!
PLAP
CRK!
UNFORTUNATELY, SHE HAS NOT.

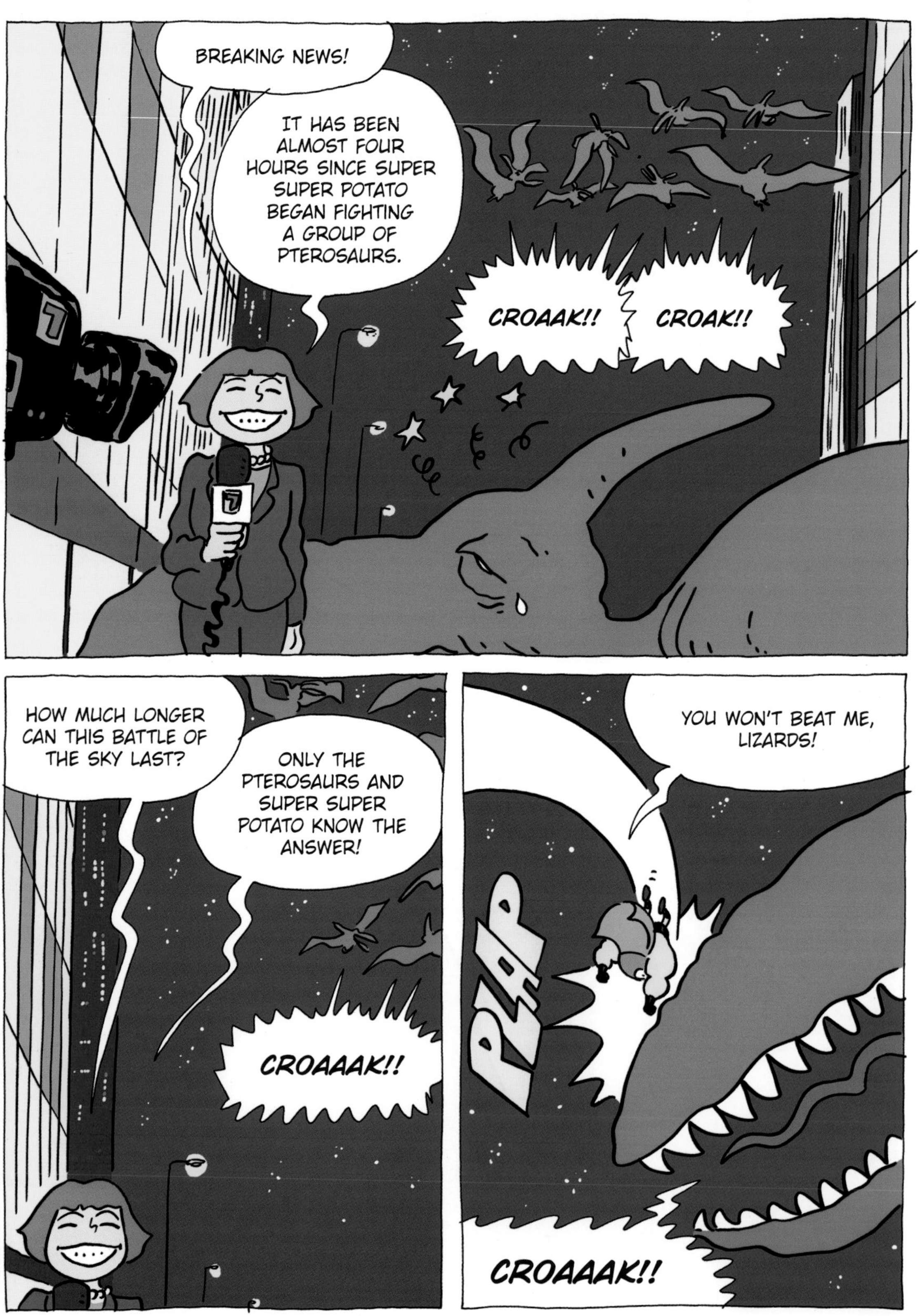
BREAKING NEWS!
IT HAS BEEN ALMOST FOUR HOURS SINCE SUPER SUPER POTATO BEGAN FIGHTING A GROUP OF PTEROSAURS.
CROAAK!!
CROAK!!
HOW MUCH LONGER CAN THIS BATTLE OF THE SKY LAST?
ONLY THE PTEROSAURS AND SUPER SUPER POTATO KNOW THE ANSWER!
CROAAAK!!
YOU WON'T BEAT ME, LIZARDS!
PLAP
CROAAAK!!

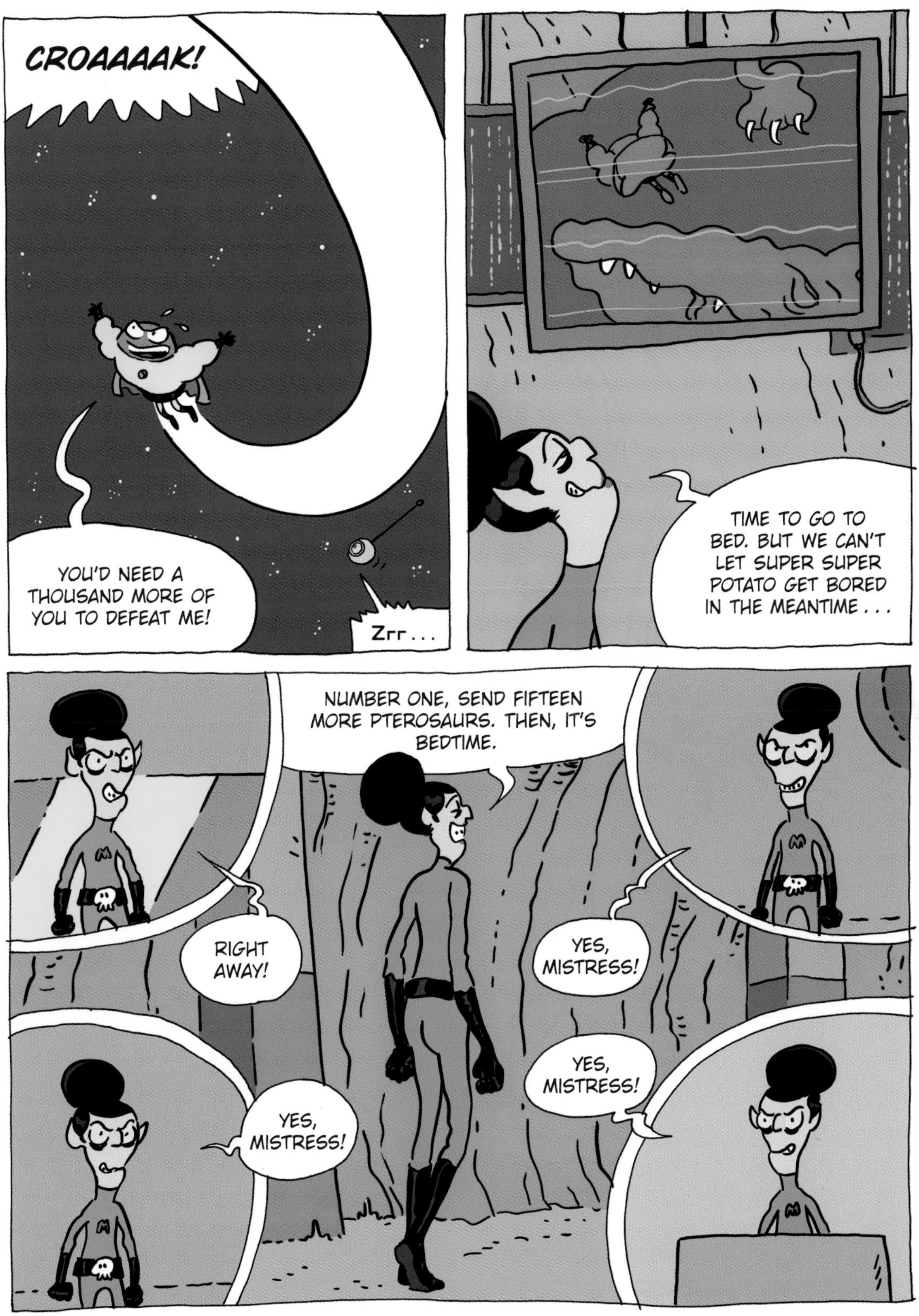
CROAAAAK!
YOU'D NEED A THOUSAND MORE OF YOU TO DEFEAT ME!
Zrr . . .
TIME TO GO TO BED. BUT WE CAN'T LET SUPER SUPER POTATO GET BORED IN THE MEANTIME . . .
NUMBER ONE, SEND FIFTEEN MORE PTEROSAURS. THEN, IT'S BEDTIME.
RIGHT AWAY!
YES, MISTRESS!
YES, MISTRESS!
YES, MISTRESS!

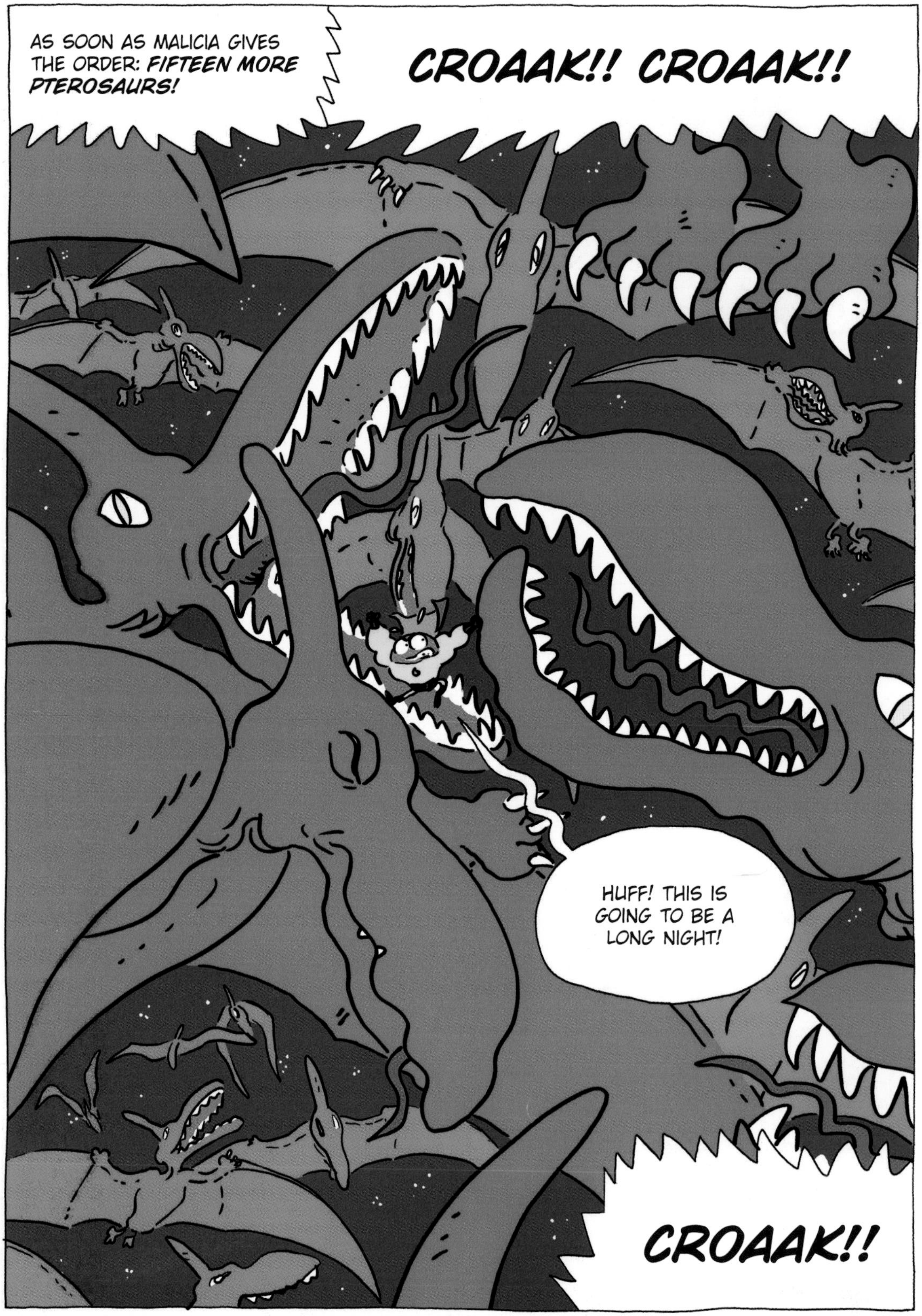
AS SOON AS MALICIA GIVES THE ORDER: *FIFTEEN MORE PTEROSAURS!*
CROAAK!! CROAAK!!
HUFF! THIS IS GOING TO BE A LONG NIGHT!
CROAAK!!

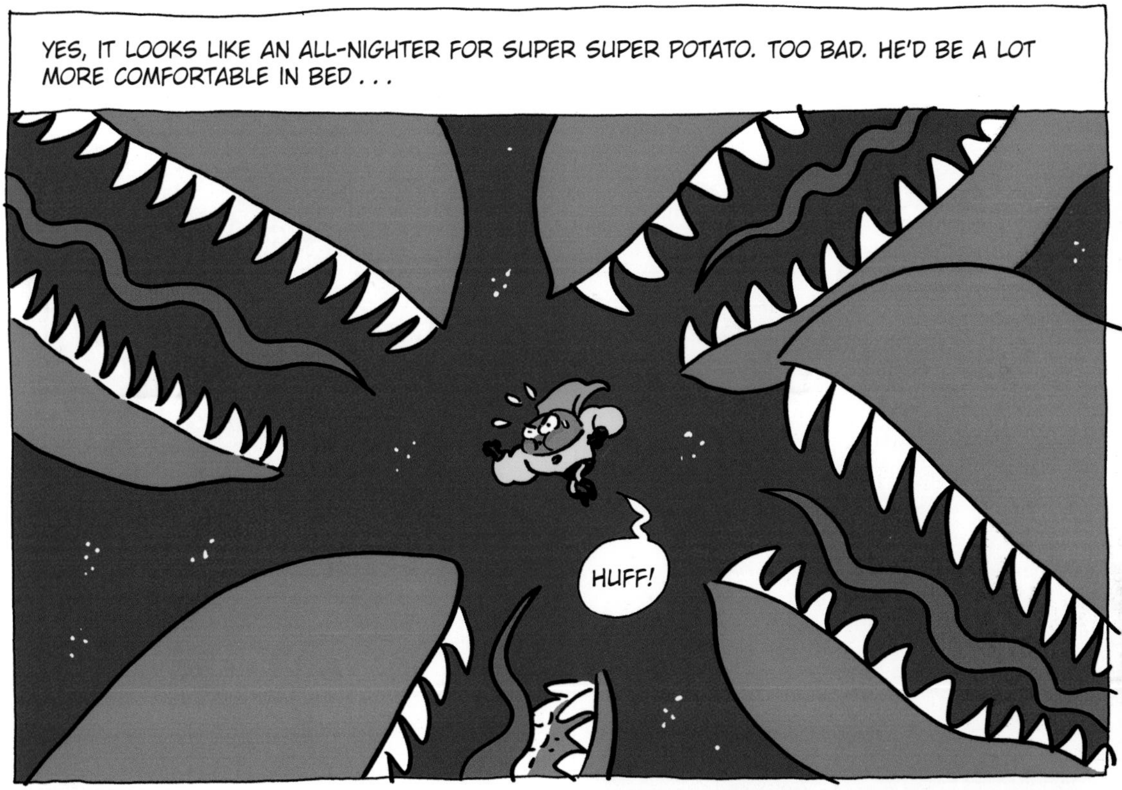
YES, IT LOOKS LIKE AN ALL-NIGHTER FOR SUPER SUPER POTATO. TOO BAD. HE'D BE A LOT MORE COMFORTABLE IN BED . . .
HUFF!

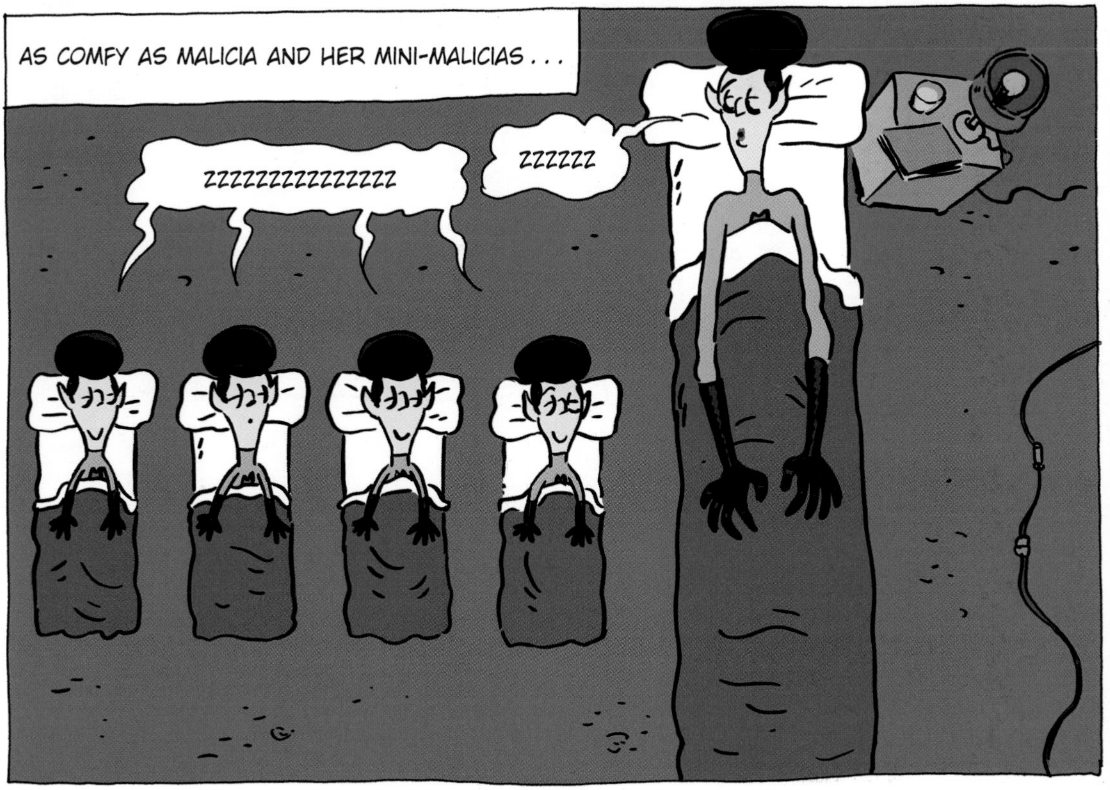
AS COMFY AS MALICIA AND HER MINI-MALICIAS . . .
ZZZZZZZZZZZZZZZZ
ZZZZZZ

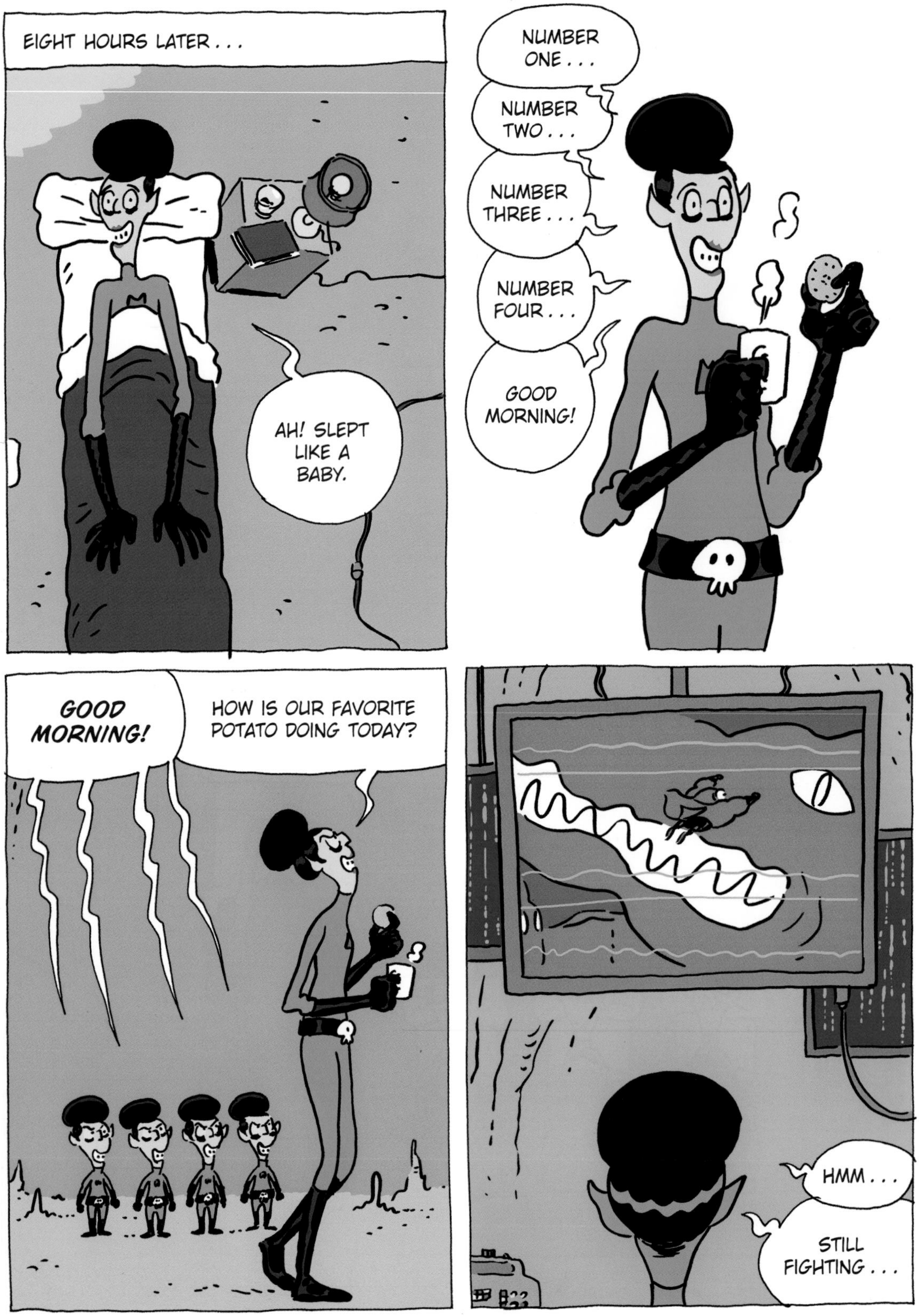
EIGHT HOURS LATER . . .
AH! SLEPT LIKE A BABY.
NUMBER ONE . . .
NUMBER TWO . . .
NUMBER THREE . . .
NUMBER FOUR . . .
GOOD MORNING!
GOOD MORNING!
HOW IS OUR FAVORITE POTATO DOING TODAY?
HMM . . .
STILL FIGHTING . . .

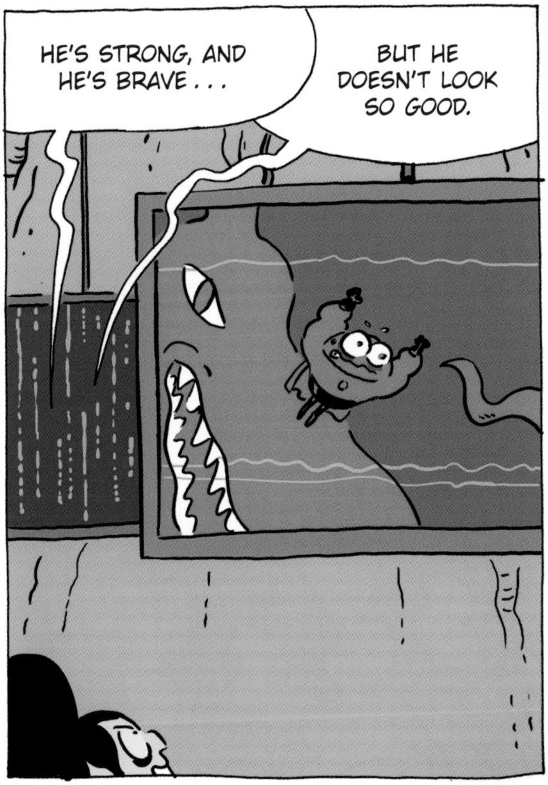
HE'S STRONG, AND HE'S BRAVE . . .
BUT HE DOESN'T LOOK SO GOOD.

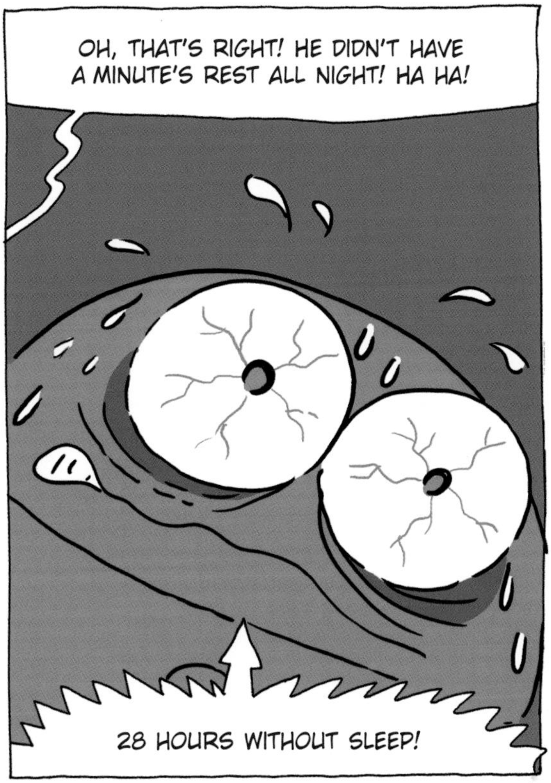
OH, THAT'S RIGHT! HE DIDN'T HAVE A MINUTE'S REST ALL NIGHT! HA HA!
28 HOURS WITHOUT SLEEP!

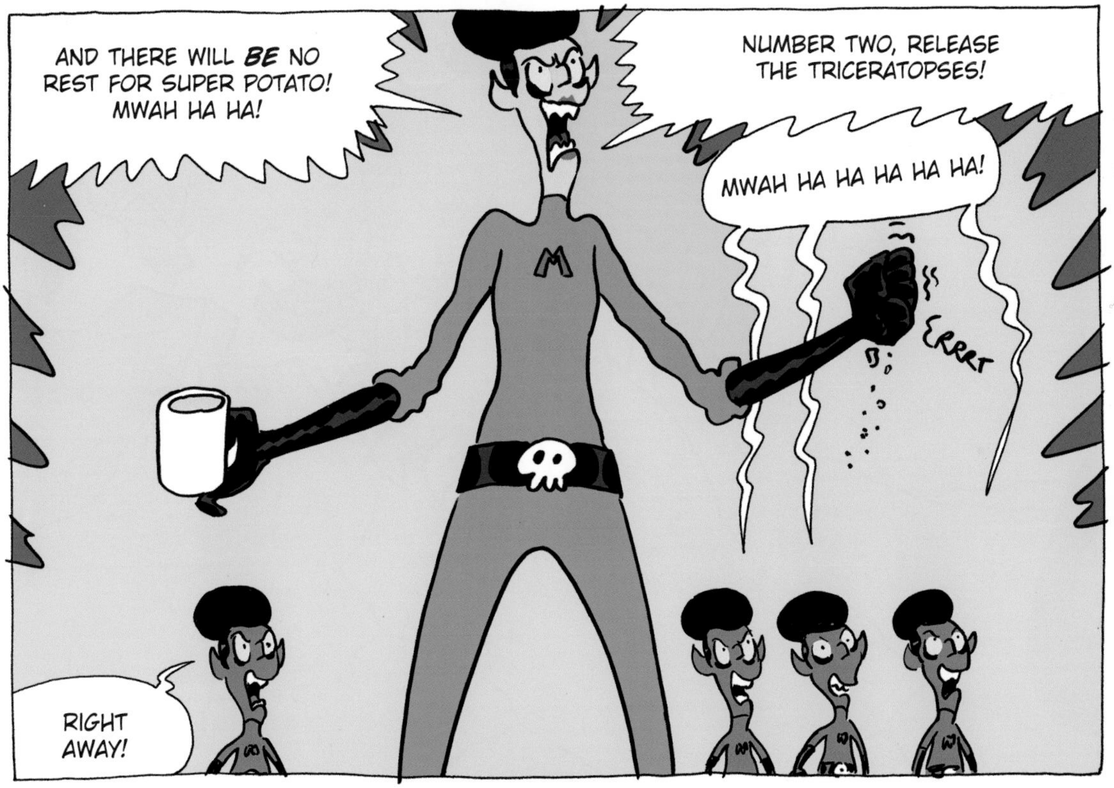
AND THERE WILL ***BE*** NO REST FOR SUPER POTATO! MWAH HA HA!
NUMBER TWO, RELEASE THE TRICERATOPSES!
MWAH HA HA HA HA HA!
RIGHT AWAY!
ERRRT

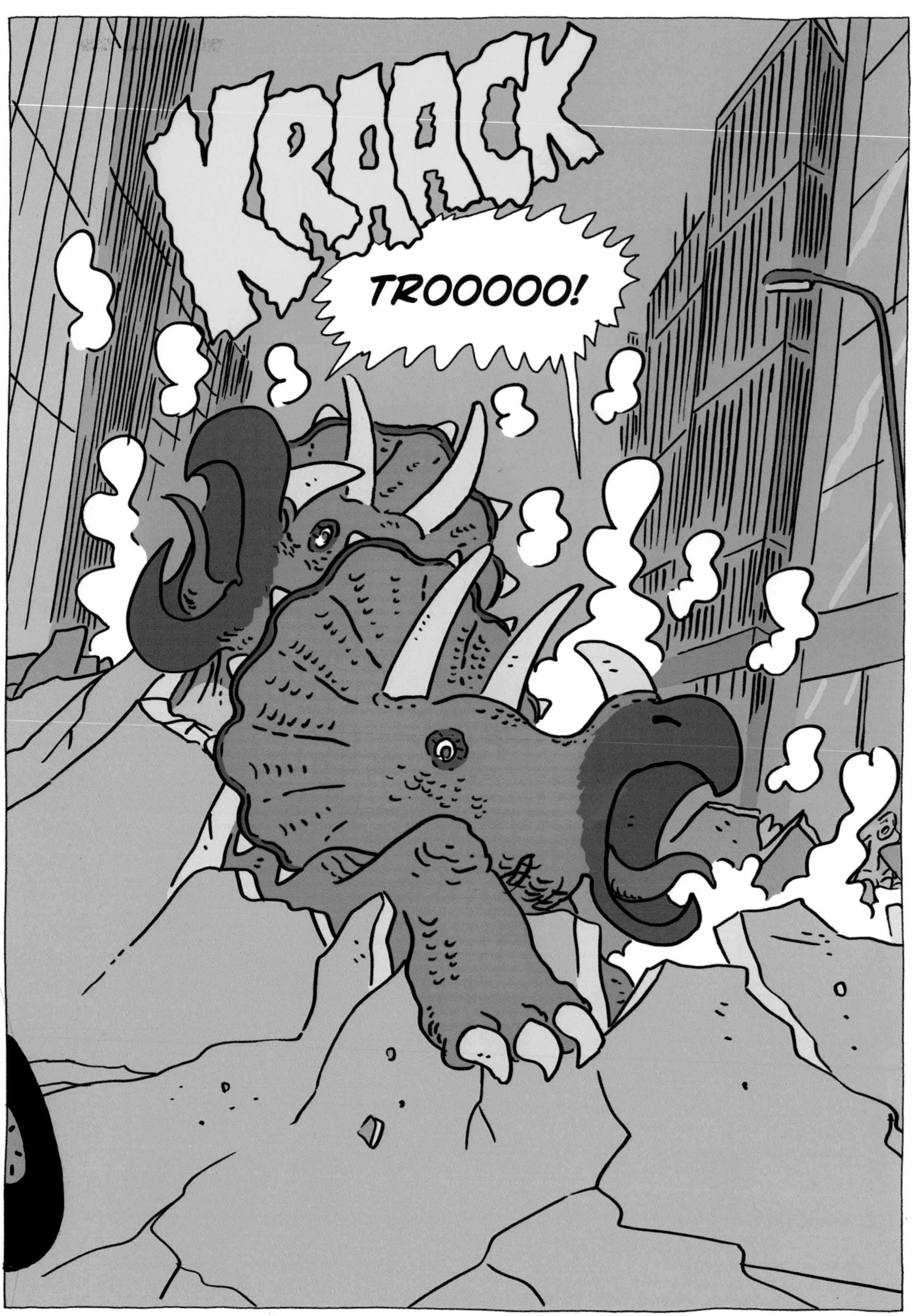
KRACK
TROOOOO!

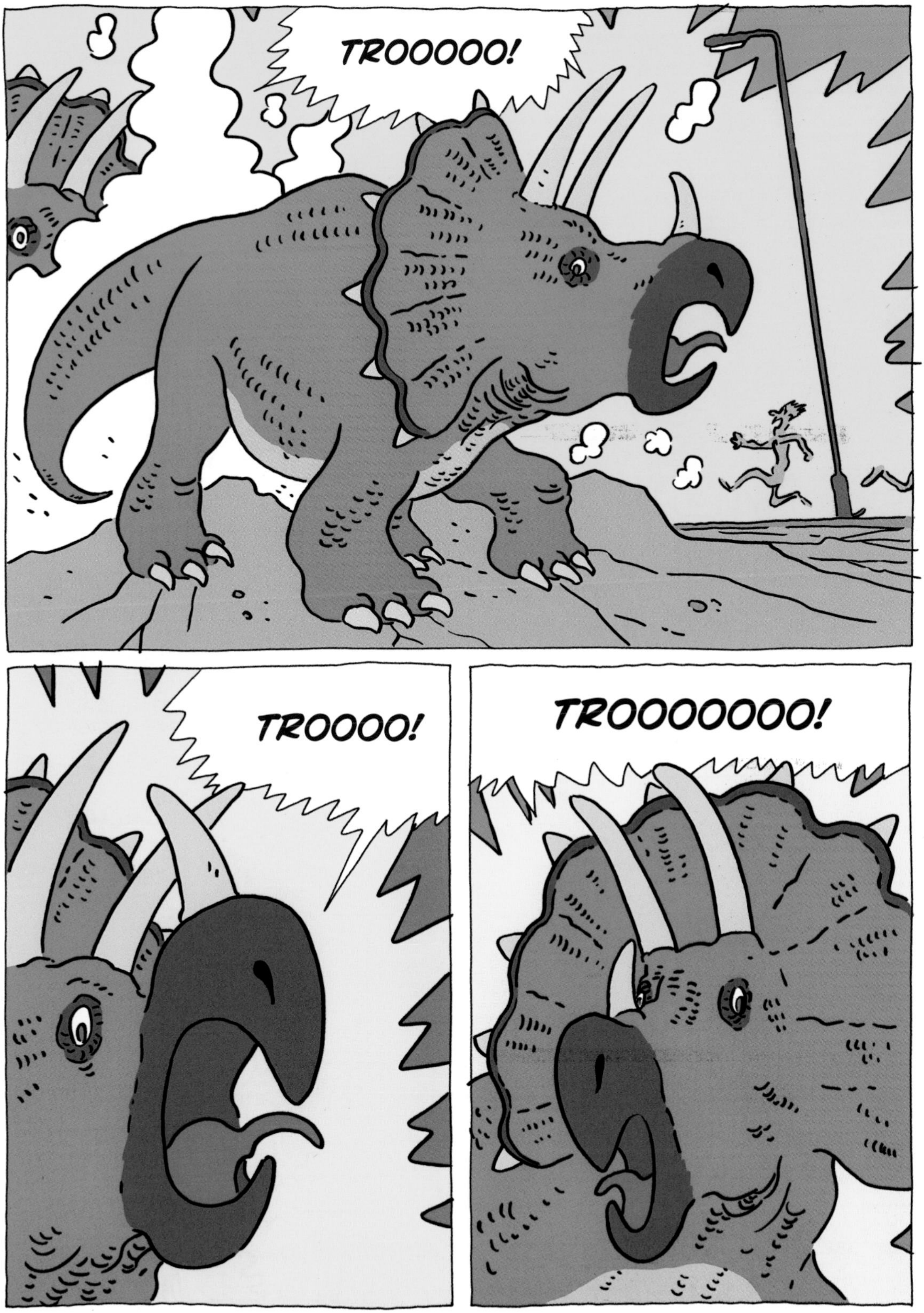
TROOOOO!
TROOOO!
TROOOOOOOO!

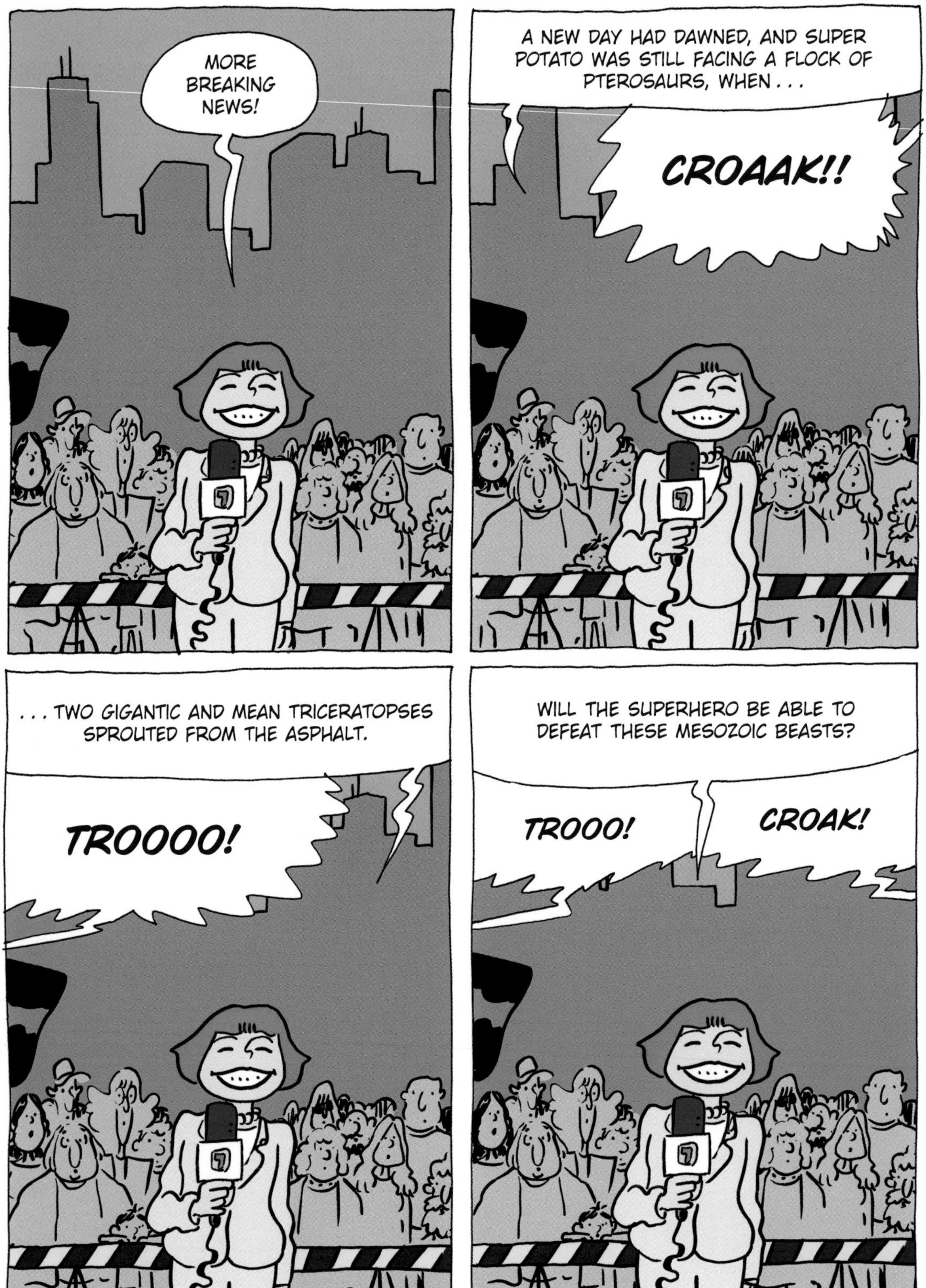
MORE BREAKING NEWS!
A NEW DAY HAD DAWNED, AND SUPER POTATO WAS STILL FACING A FLOCK OF PTEROSAURS, WHEN . . .
CROAAK!!
. . . TWO GIGANTIC AND MEAN TRICERATOPSES SPROUTED FROM THE ASPHALT.
TROOOO!
WILL THE SUPERHERO BE ABLE TO DEFEAT THESE MESOZOIC BEASTS?
TROOO!
CROAK!

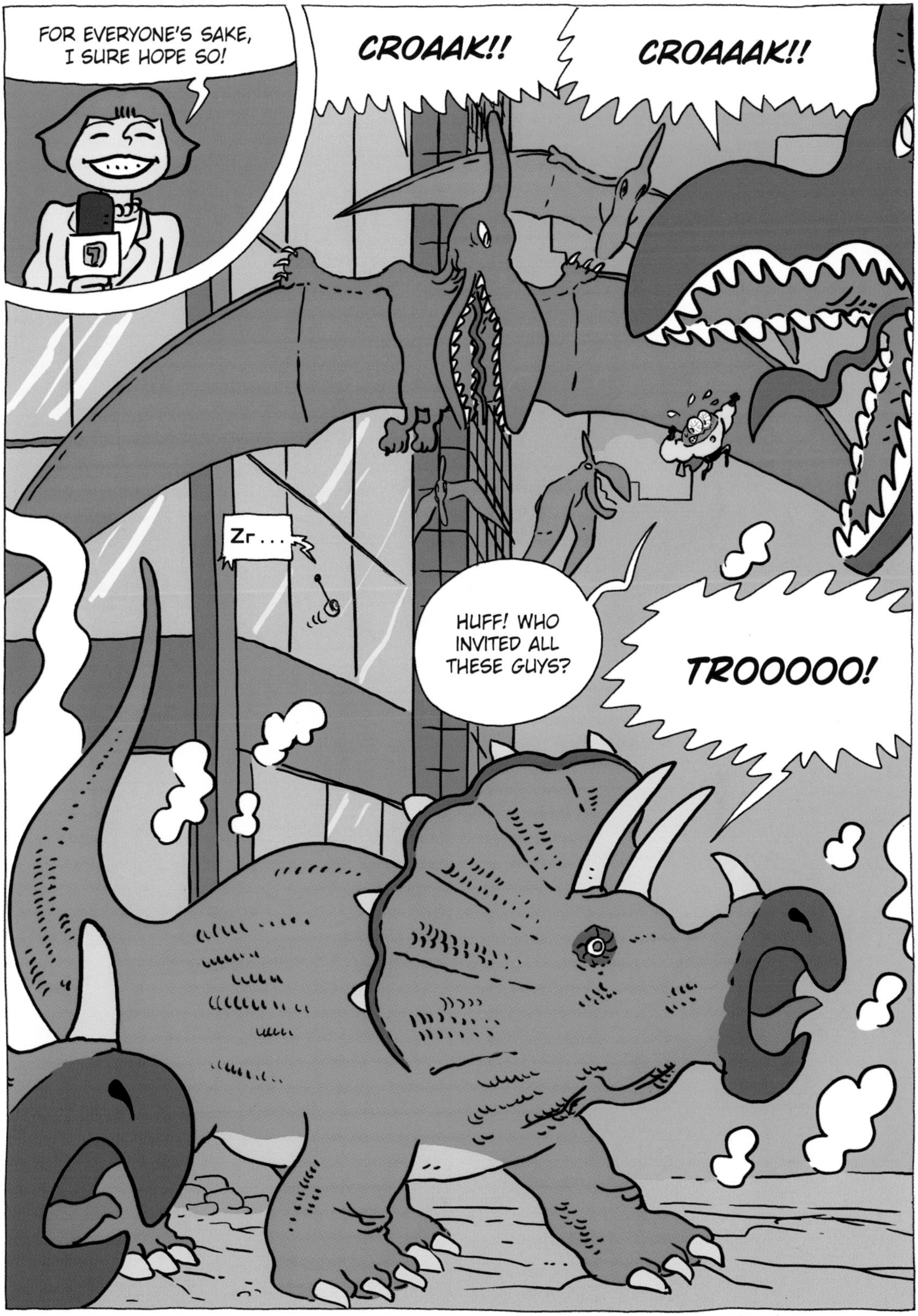
FOR EVERYONE'S SAKE, I SURE HOPE SO!
CROAAK!!
CROAAAK!!
Zr . . .
HUFF! WHO INVITED ALL THESE GUYS?
TROOOOO!

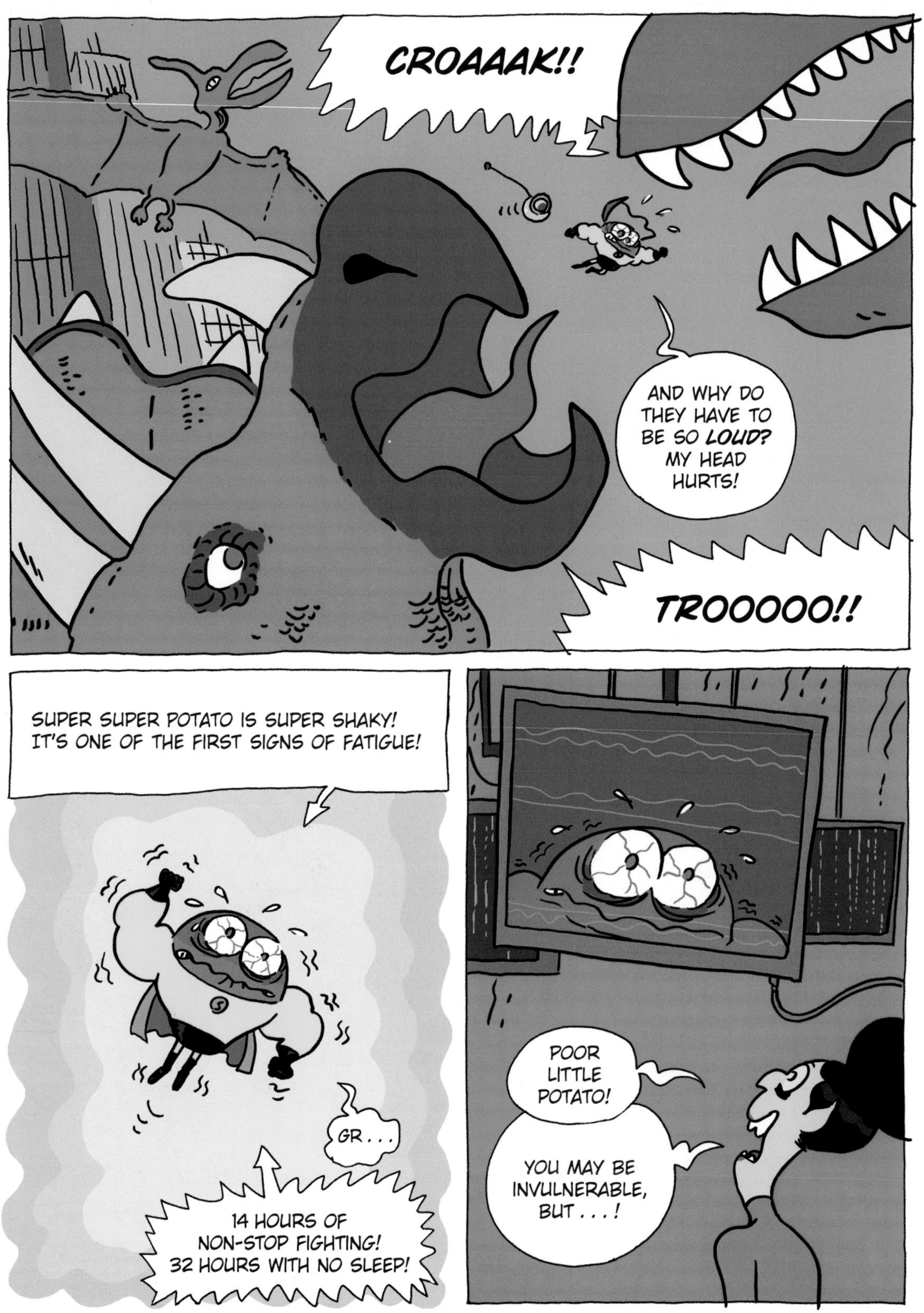
CROAAAK!!
AND WHY DO THEY HAVE TO BE SO LOUD? MY HEAD HURTS!
TROOOOO!!
SUPER SUPER POTATO IS SUPER SHAKY! IT'S ONE OF THE FIRST SIGNS OF FATIGUE!
GR . . .
14 HOURS OF NON-STOP FIGHTING! 32 HOURS WITH NO SLEEP!
POOR LITTLE POTATO!
YOU MAY BE INVULNERABLE, BUT . . . !

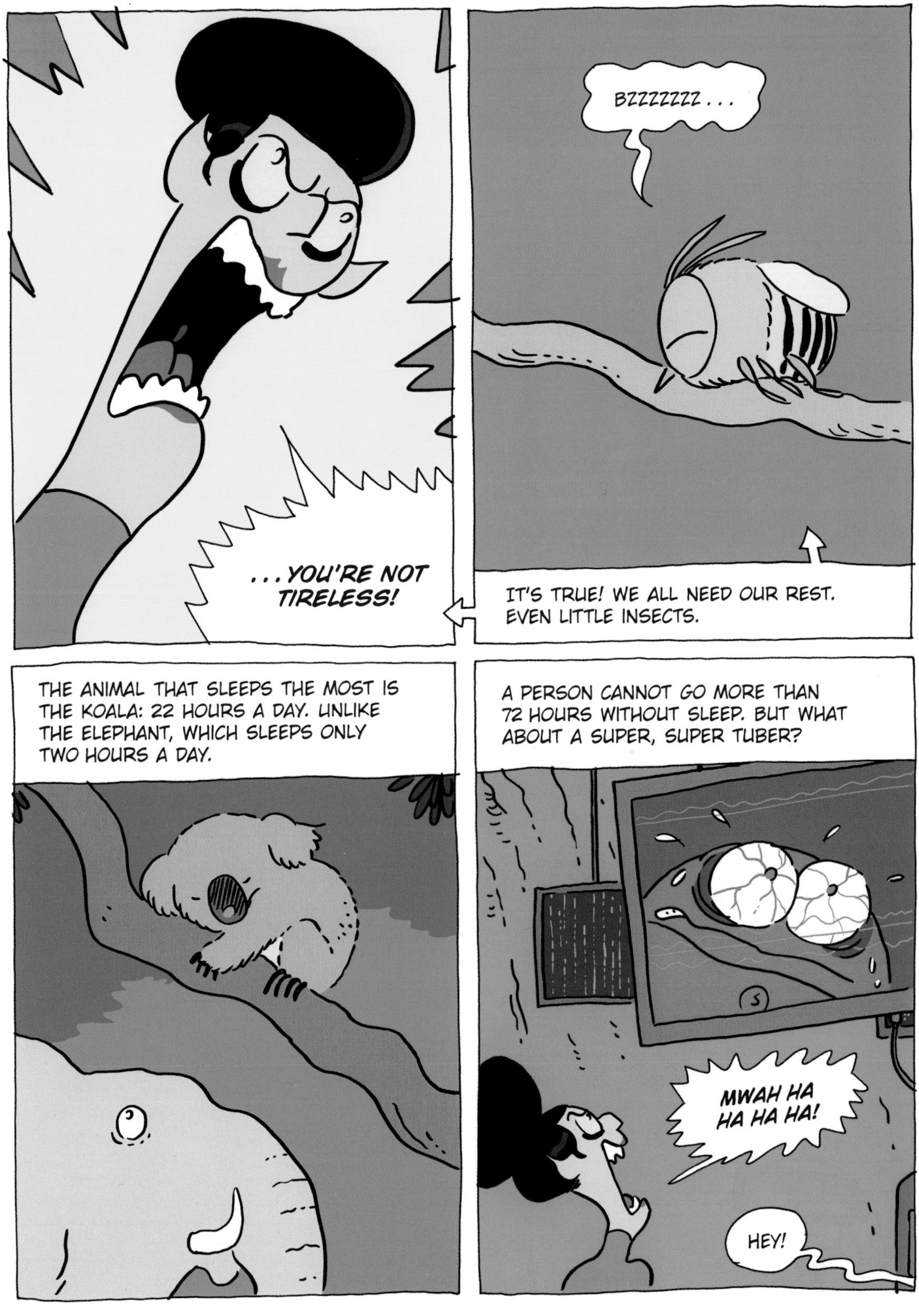

. . . YOU'RE NOT TIRELESS!
BZZZZZZZ . . .
IT'S TRUE! WE ALL NEED OUR REST. EVEN LITTLE INSECTS.
THE ANIMAL THAT SLEEPS THE MOST IS THE KOALA: 22 HOURS A DAY. UNLIKE THE ELEPHANT, WHICH SLEEPS ONLY TWO HOURS A DAY.
A PERSON CANNOT GO MORE THAN 72 HOURS WITHOUT SLEEP. BUT WHAT ABOUT A SUPER, SUPER TUBER?
MWAH HA HA HA HA!
HEY!

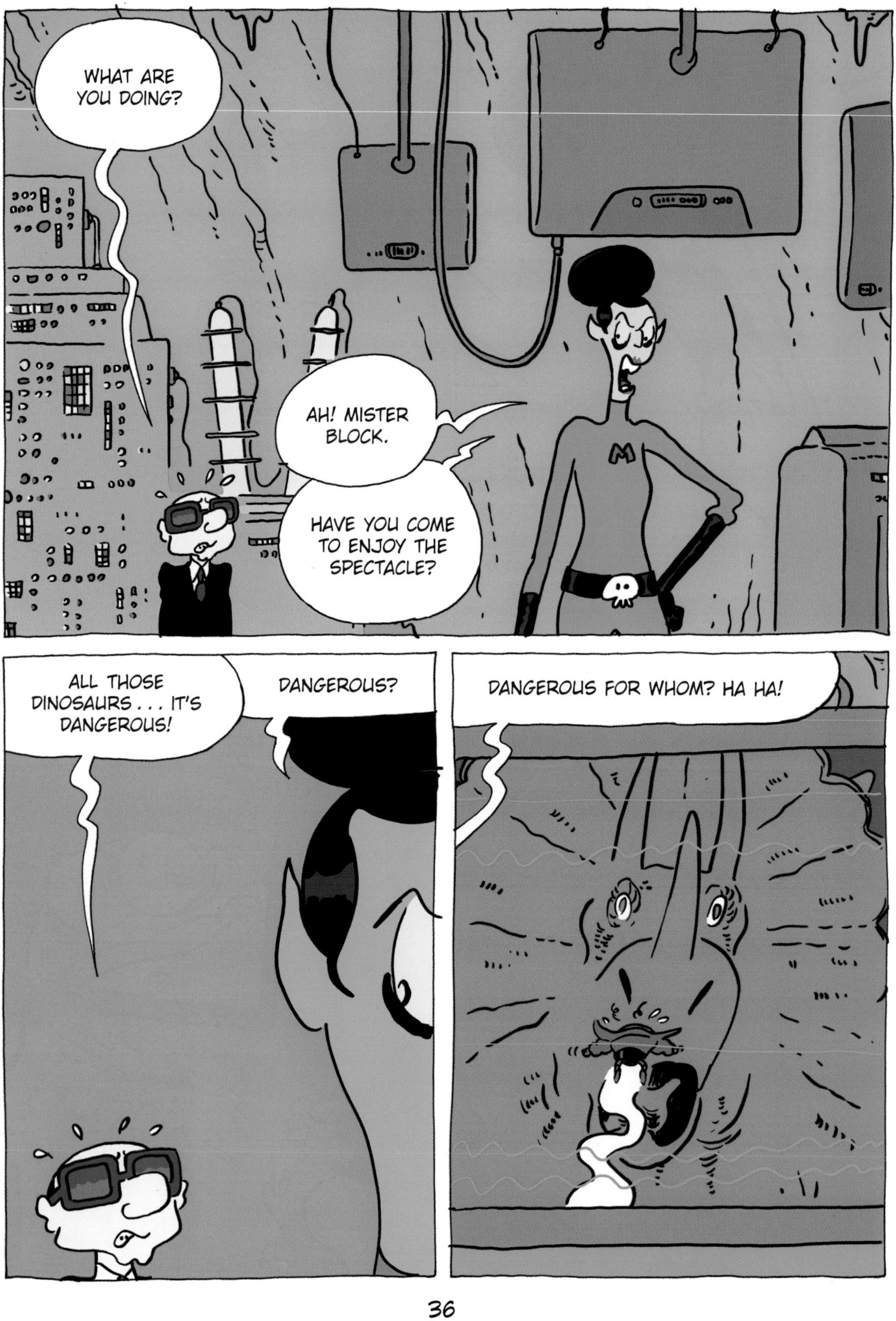

WHAT ARE YOU DOING?
AH! MISTER BLOCK.
HAVE YOU COME TO ENJOY THE SPECTACLE?
ALL THOSE DINOSAURS . . . IT'S DANGEROUS!
DANGEROUS?
DANGEROUS FOR WHOM? HA HA!

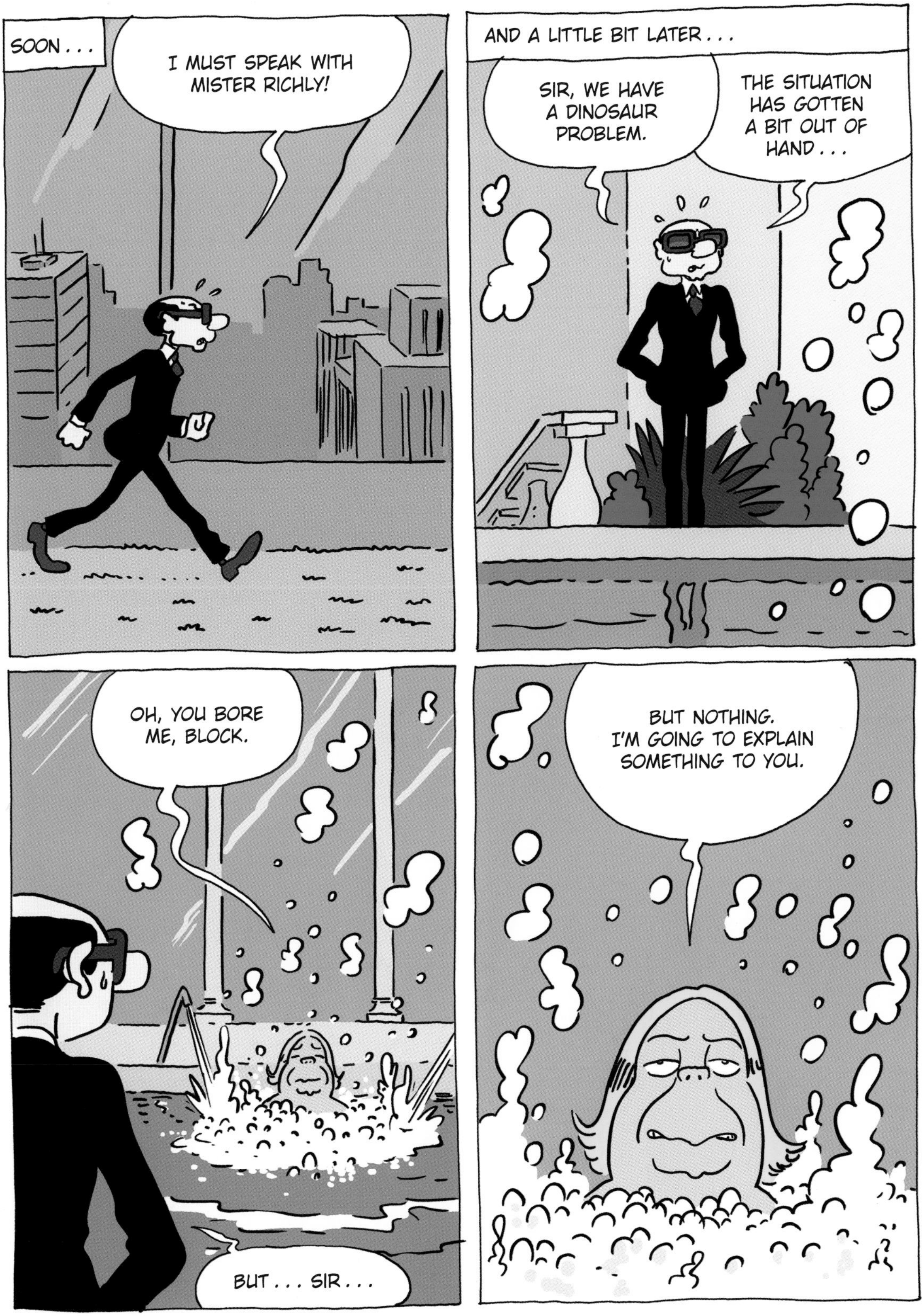
SOON . . .
I MUST SPEAK WITH MISTER RICHLY!
AND A LITTLE BIT LATER . . .
SIR, WE HAVE A DINOSAUR PROBLEM.
THE SITUATION HAS GOTTEN A BIT OUT OF HAND . . .
OH, YOU BORE ME, BLOCK.
BUT . . . SIR . . .
BUT NOTHING. I'M GOING TO EXPLAIN SOMETHING TO YOU.

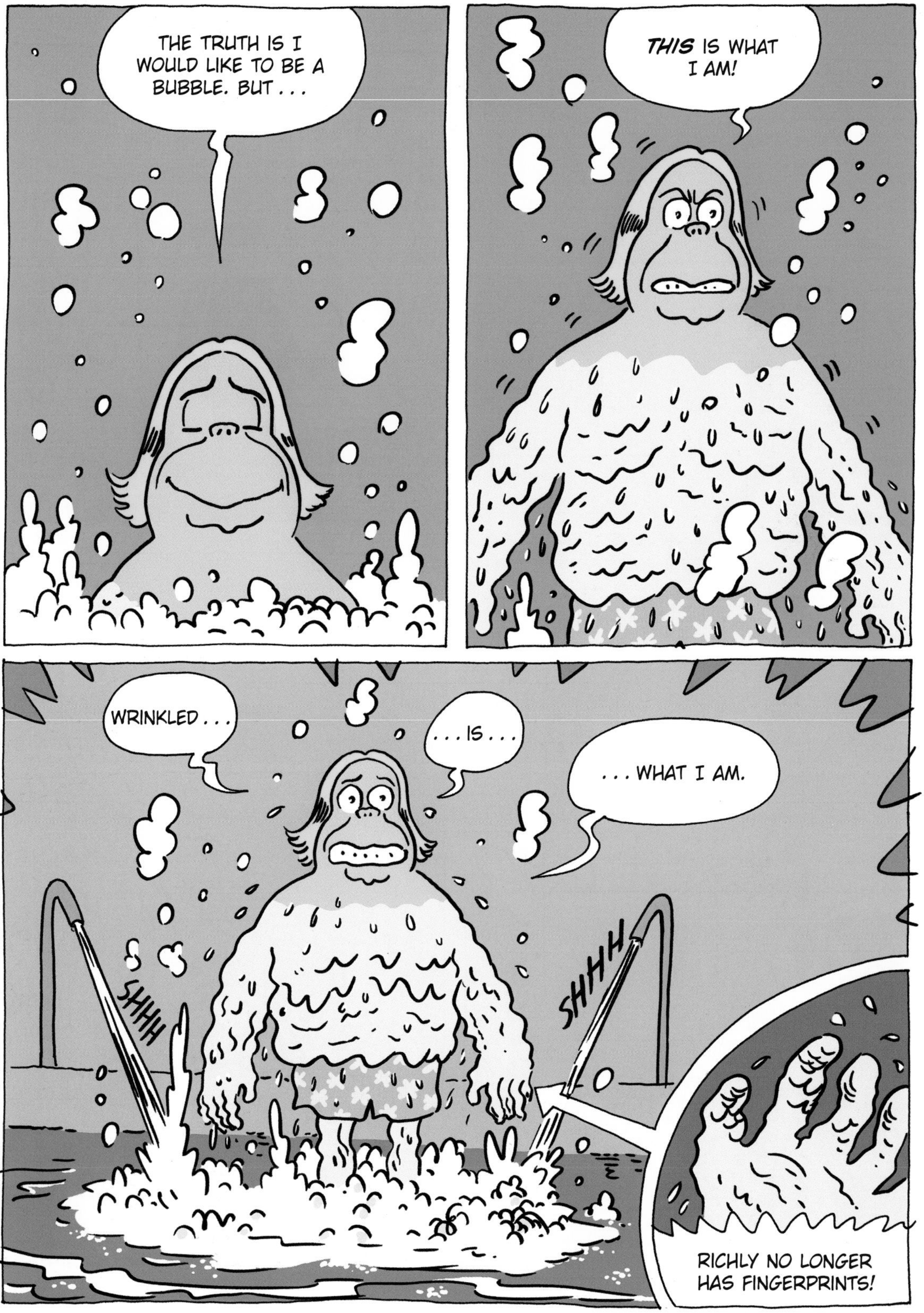
THE TRUTH IS I WOULD LIKE TO BE A BUBBLE. BUT . . .
THIS IS WHAT I AM!
WRINKLED . . .
. . . IS . . .
. . . WHAT I AM.
SHHH
SHHH
RICHLY NO LONGER HAS FINGERPRINTS!

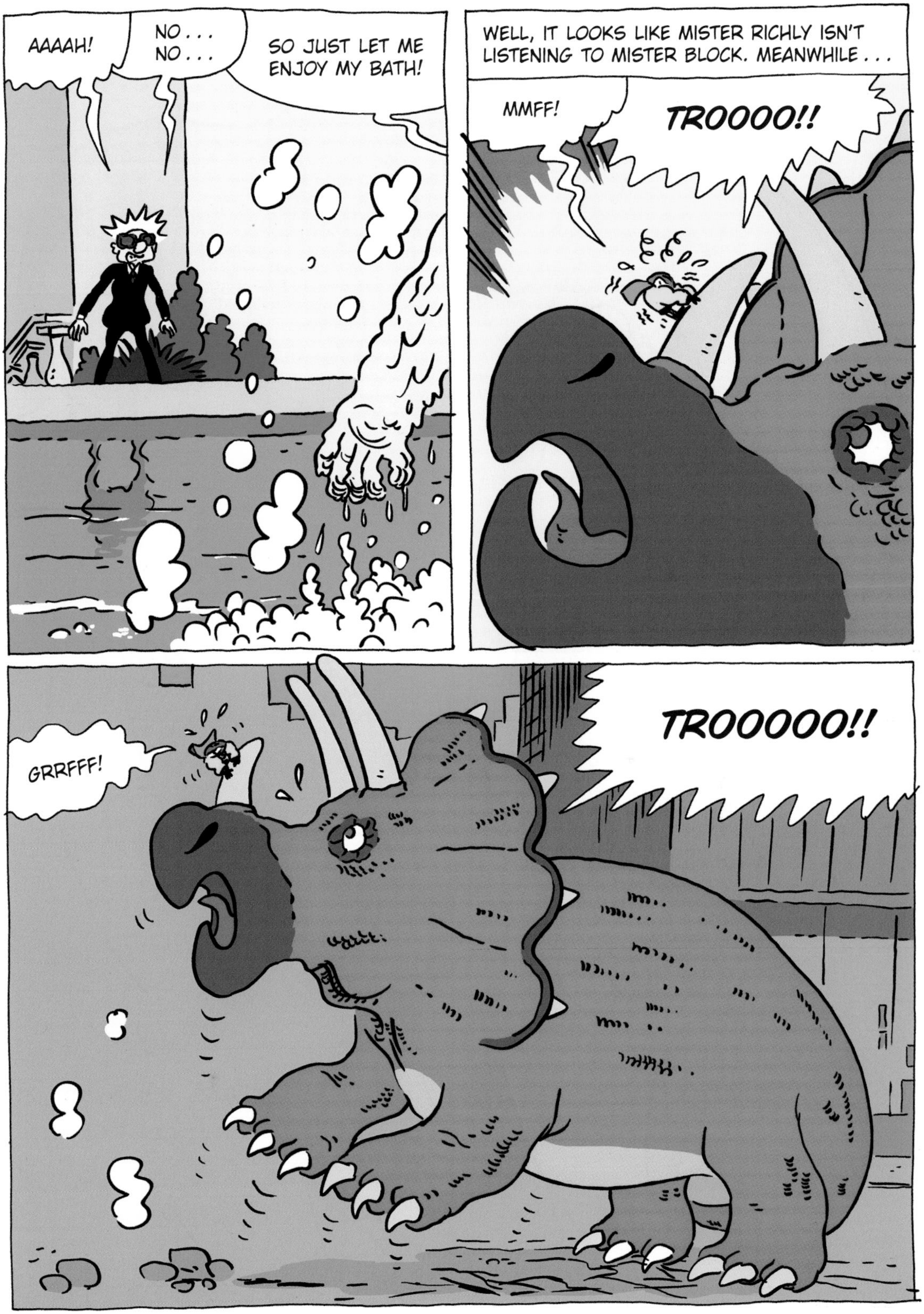
AAAAH!
NO . . .
NO . . .
SO JUST LET ME ENJOY MY BATH!
WELL, IT LOOKS LIKE MISTER RICHLY ISN'T LISTENING TO MISTER BLOCK. MEANWHILE . . .
MMFF!
TROOOO!!
GRRFFF!
TROOOOO!!

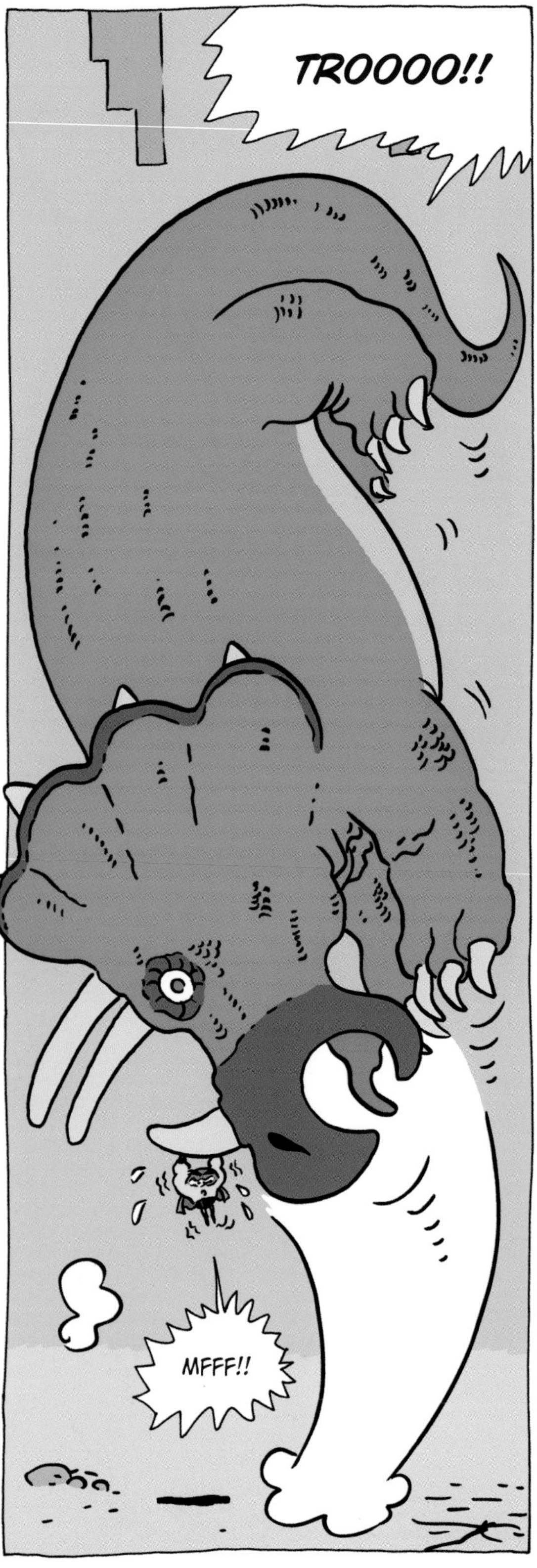
TROOOO!!
MFFF!!

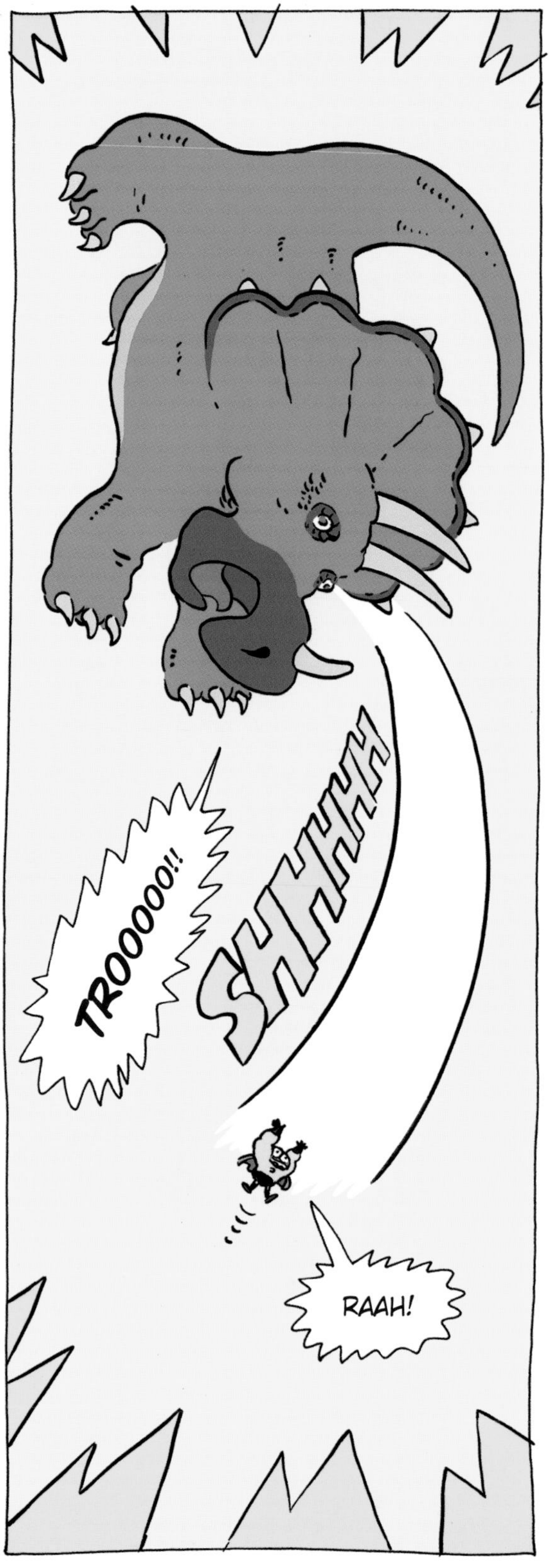
TROOOOO!!
SHHHHH
RAAH!

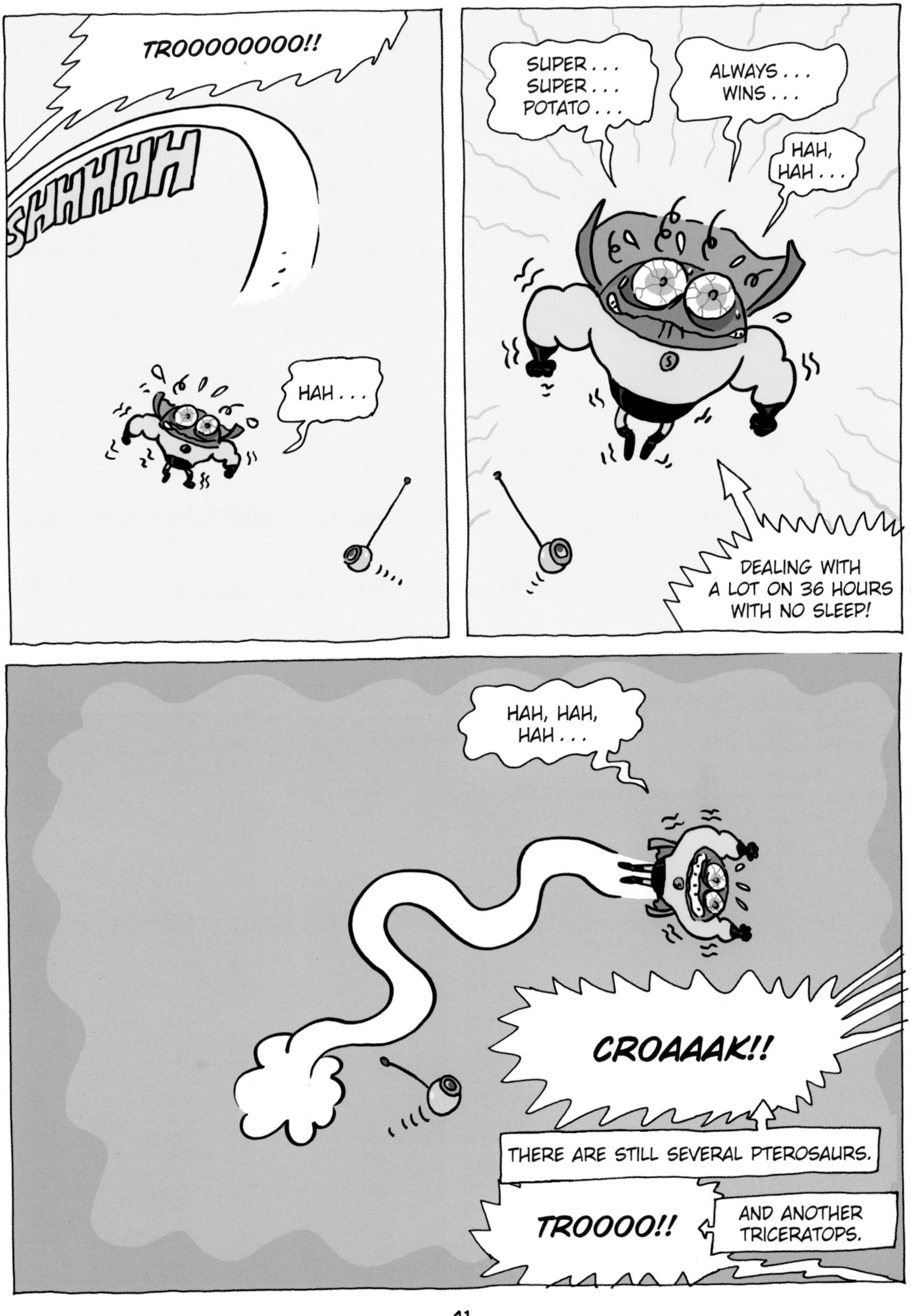
TROOOOOOOO!!
SHHHHH
HAH . . .
SUPER . . . SUPER . . . POTATO . . .
ALWAYS . . . WINS . . .
HAH, HAH . . .
DEALING WITH A LOT ON 36 HOURS WITH NO SLEEP!
HAH, HAH, HAH . . .
CROAAAK!!
THERE ARE STILL SEVERAL PTEROSAURS.
TROOOO!!
AND ANOTHER TRICERATOPS.

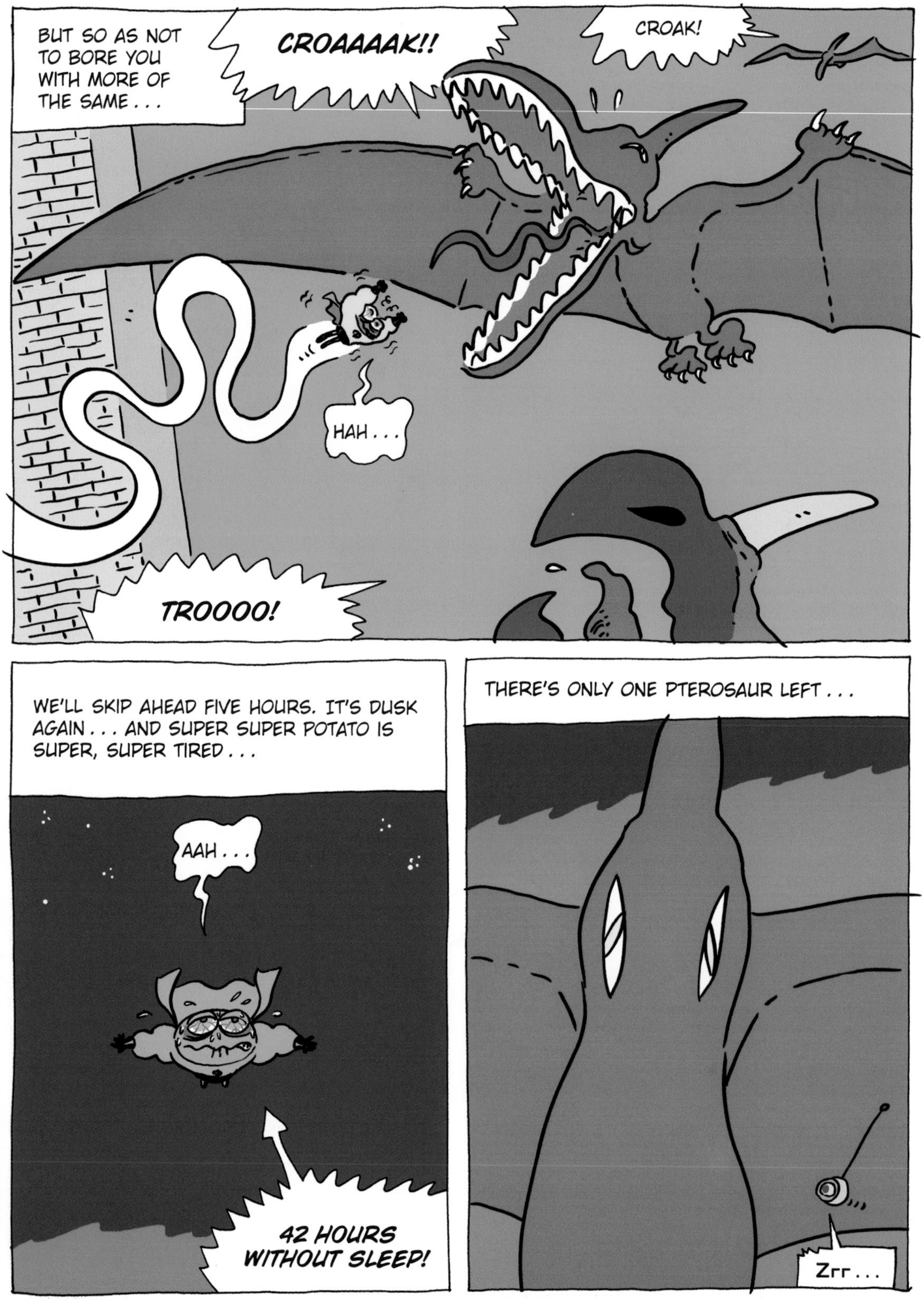

BUT SO AS NOT TO BORE YOU WITH MORE OF THE SAME . . .
CROAAAAK!!
CROAK!
HAH . . .
TROOOO!
WE'LL SKIP AHEAD FIVE HOURS. IT'S DUSK AGAIN . . . AND SUPER SUPER POTATO IS SUPER, SUPER TIRED . . .
AAH . . .
42 HOURS WITHOUT SLEEP!
THERE'S ONLY ONE PTEROSAUR LEFT . . .
Zrr . . .

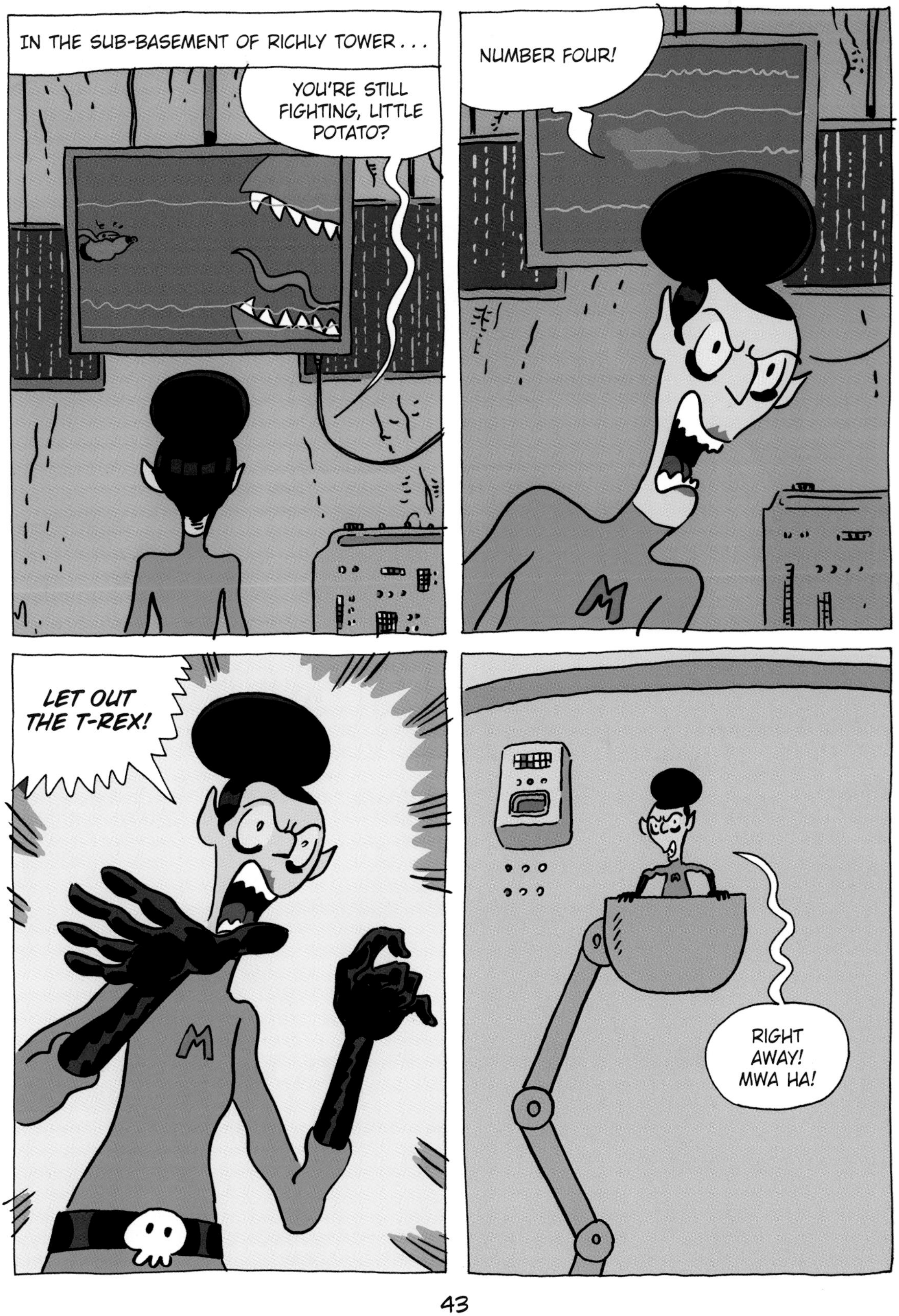
IN THE SUB-BASEMENT OF RICHLY TOWER . . .
YOU'RE STILL FIGHTING, LITTLE POTATO?
NUMBER FOUR!
LET OUT THE T-REX!
RIGHT AWAY! MWA HA!

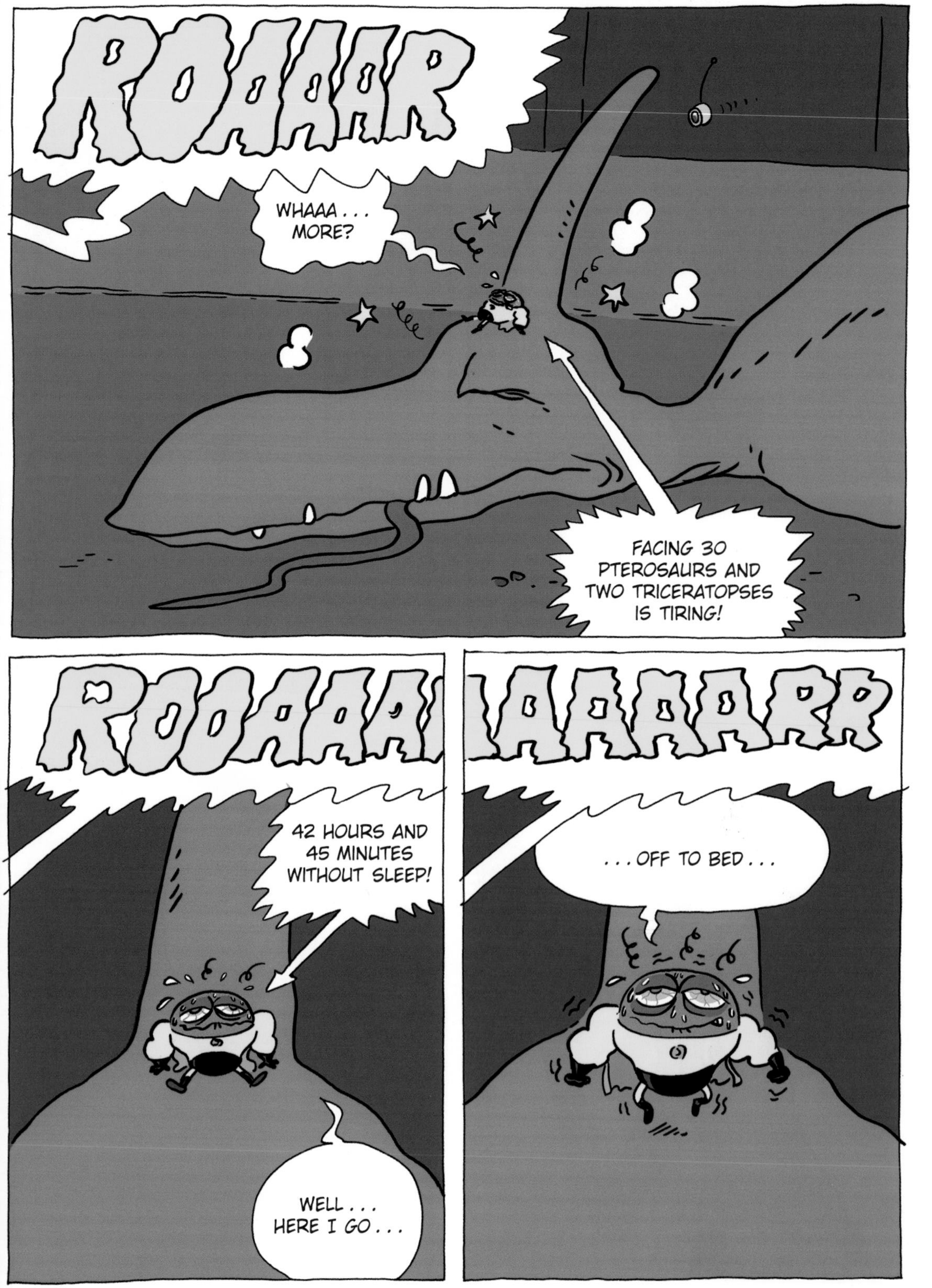
ROAAAR
WHAAA . . . MORE?
FACING 30 PTEROSAURS AND TWO TRICERATOPSES IS TIRING!
ROOAAAAAAAAARR
42 HOURS AND 45 MINUTES WITHOUT SLEEP!
WELL . . . HERE I GO . . .
. . . OFF TO BED . . .

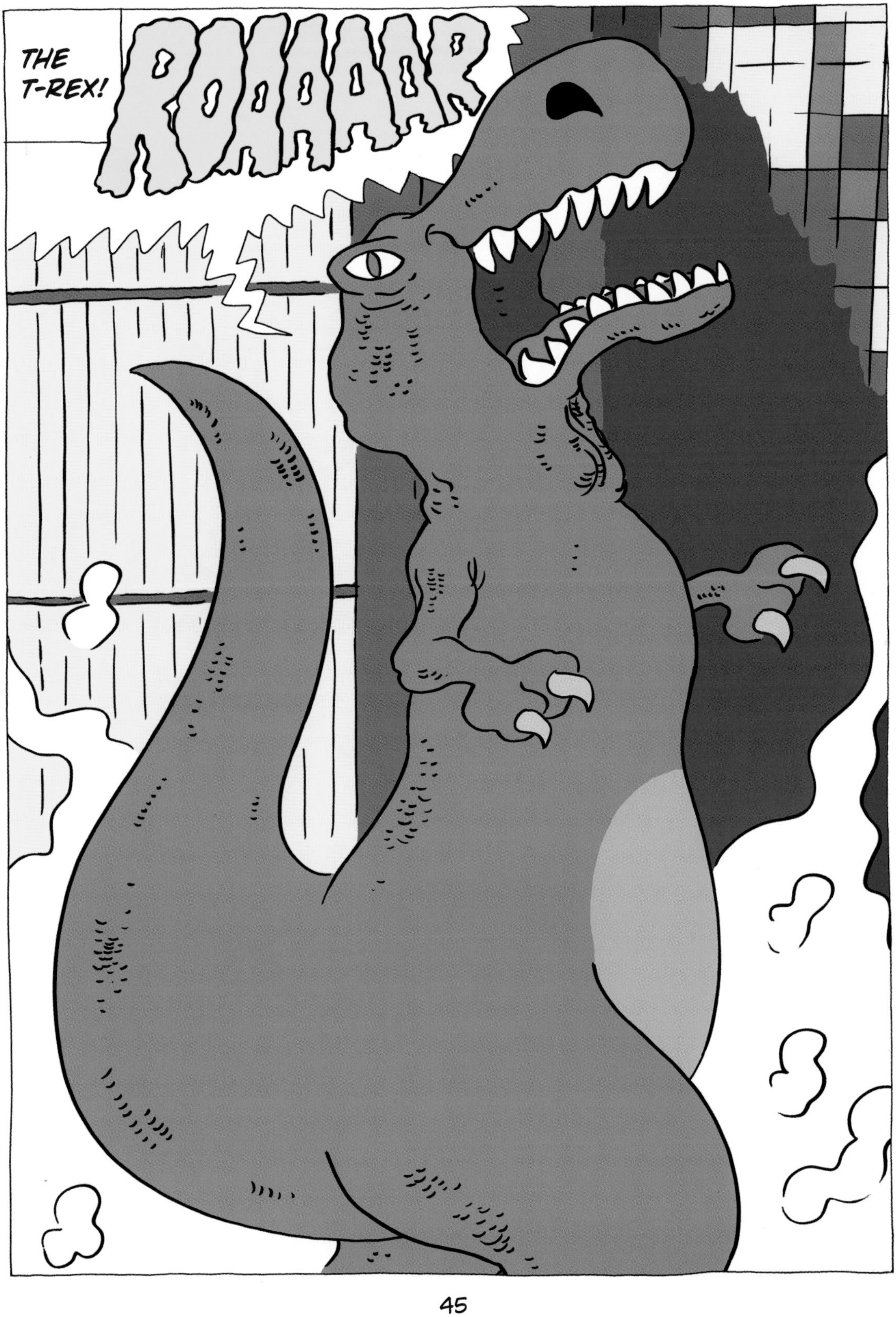
THE T-REX!
ROAAAAR

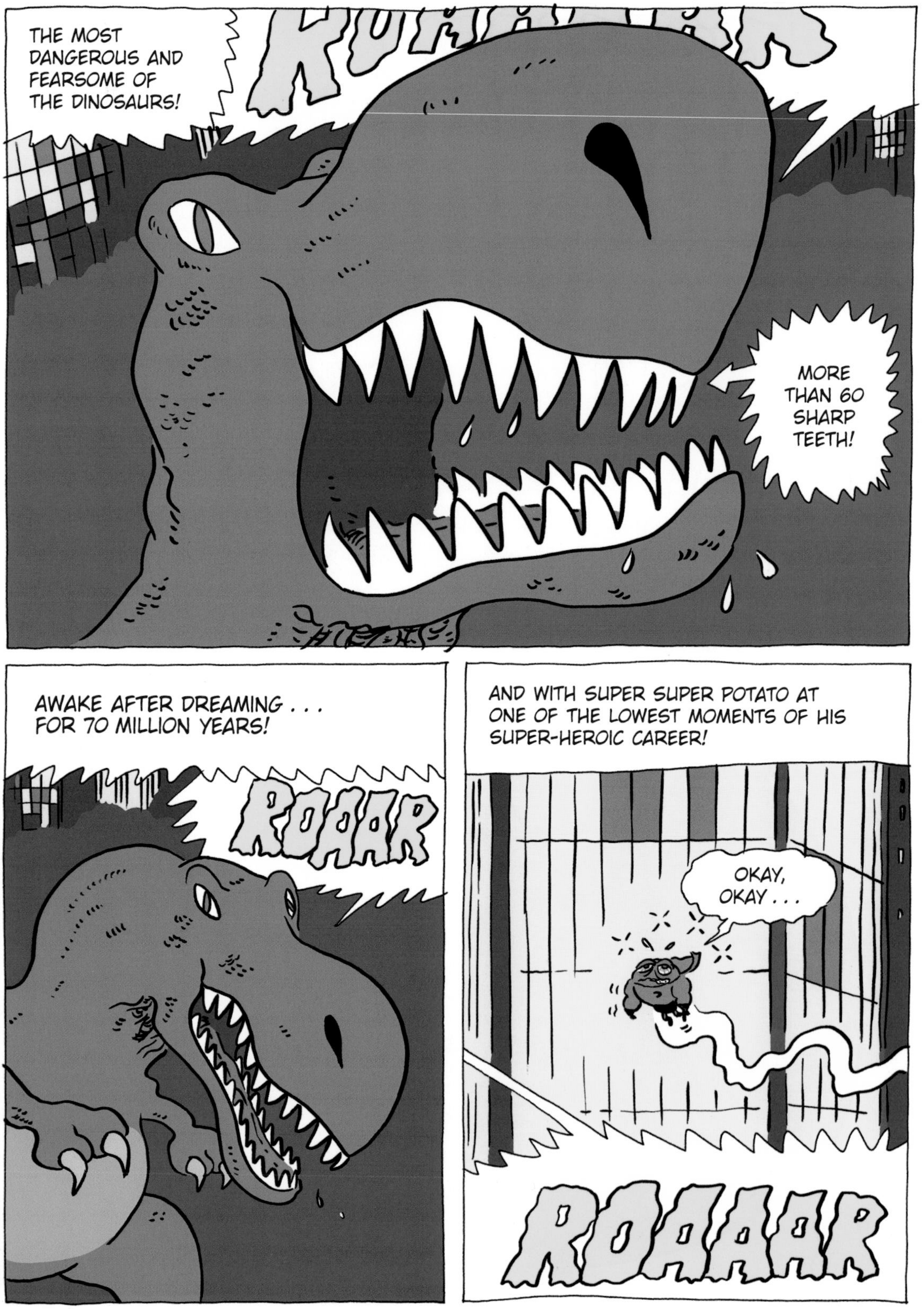
THE MOST DANGEROUS AND FEARSOME OF THE DINOSAURS!
MORE THAN 60 SHARP TEETH!
AWAKE AFTER DREAMING . . . FOR 70 MILLION YEARS!
ROAAR
AND WITH SUPER SUPER POTATO AT ONE OF THE LOWEST MOMENTS OF HIS SUPER-HEROIC CAREER!
OKAY, OKAY . . .
ROAAAR

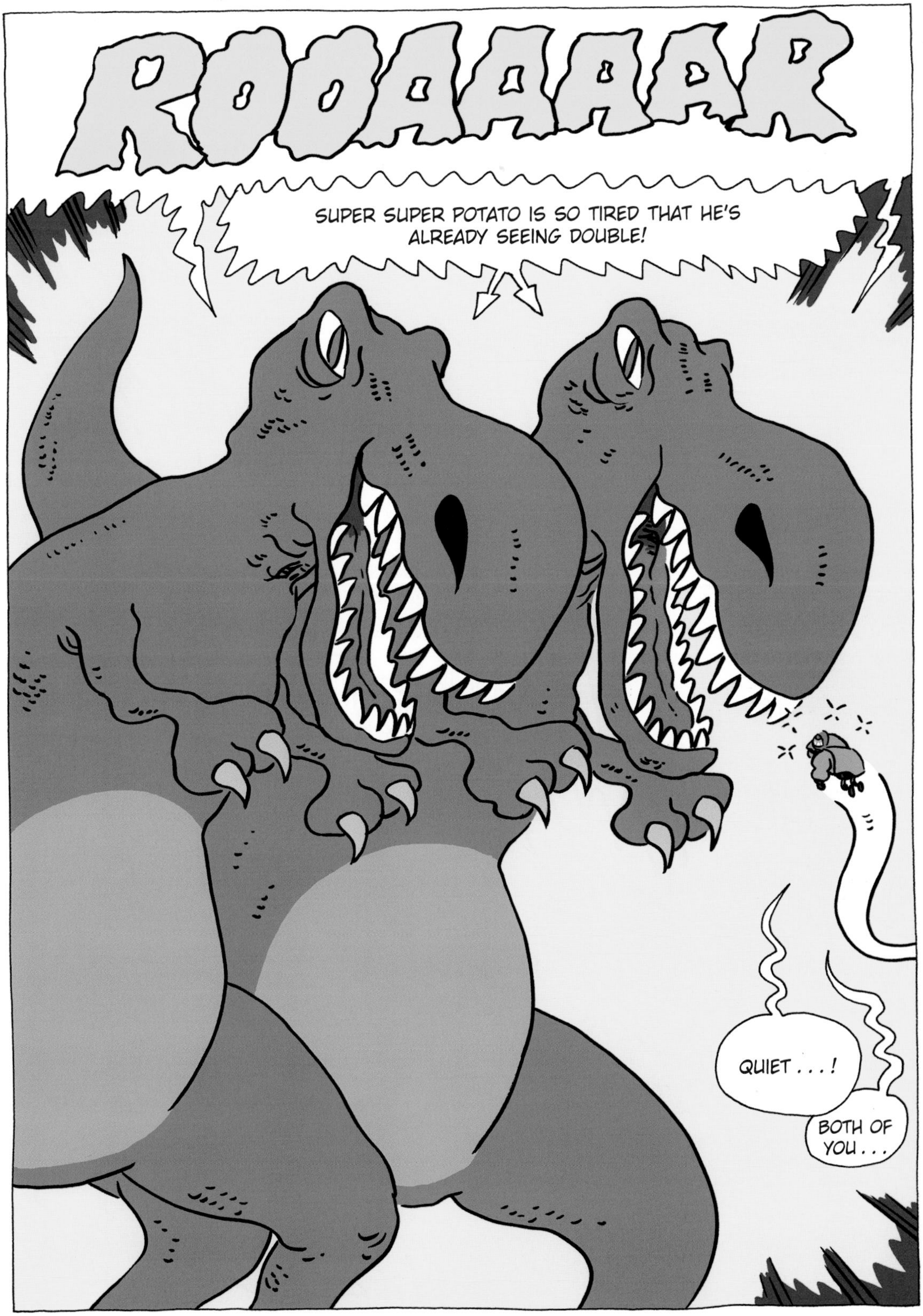
ROOAAAAR
SUPER SUPER POTATO IS SO TIRED THAT HE'S ALREADY SEEING DOUBLE!
QUIET . . . !
BOTH OF YOU . . .

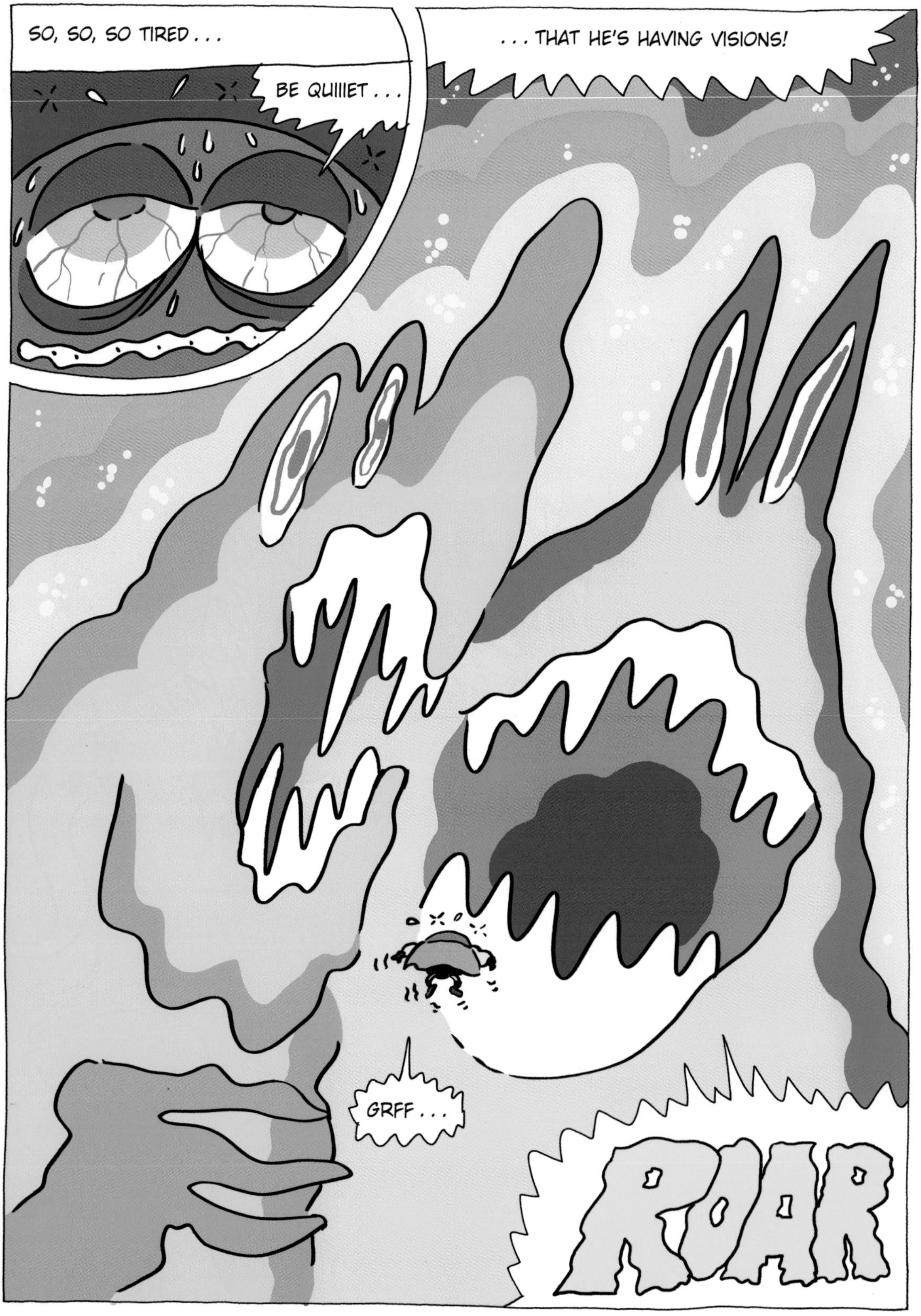
SO, SO, SO TIRED . . .
BE QUIIIET . . .
. . . THAT HE'S HAVING VISIONS!
GRFF . . .
ROAR

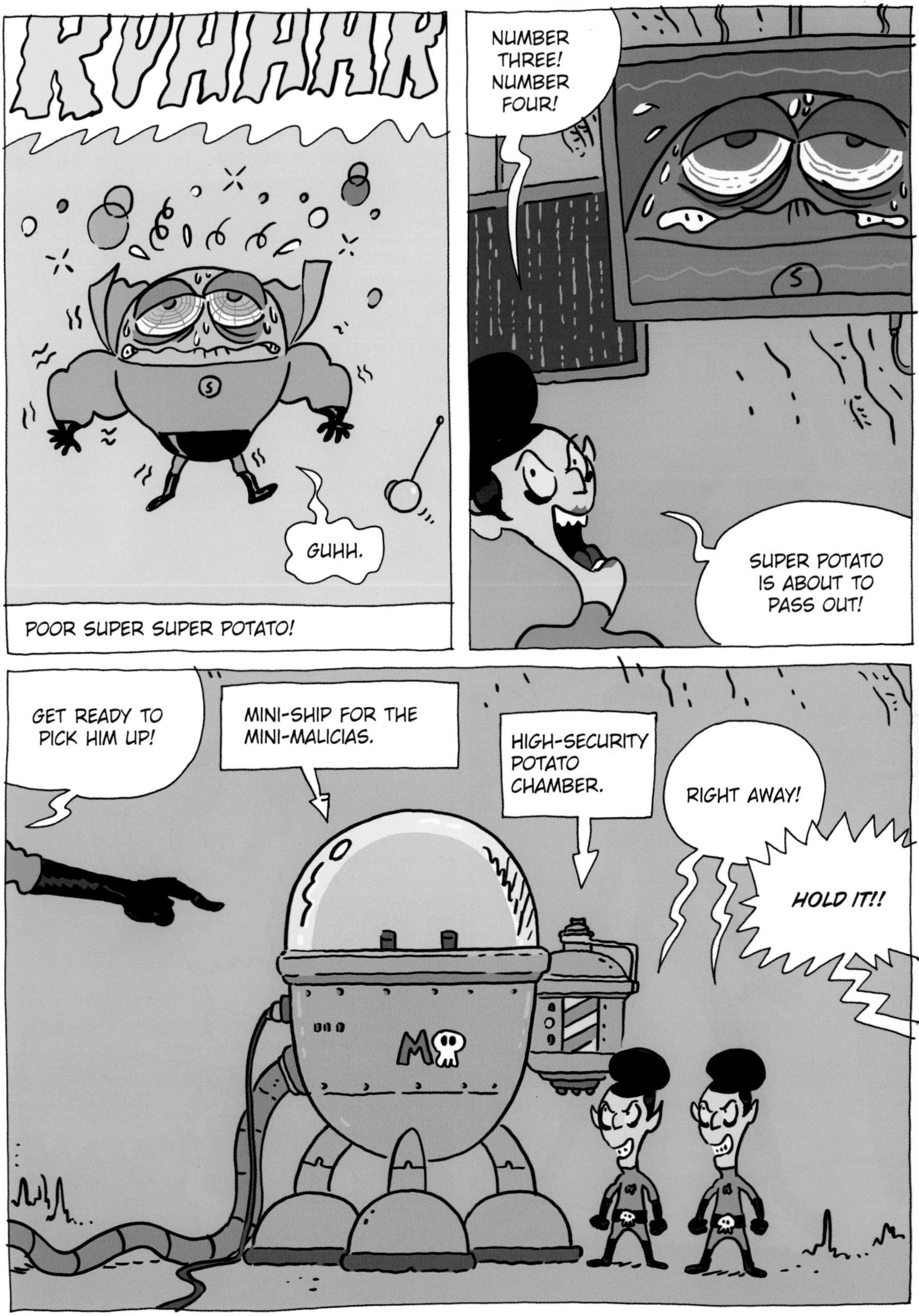
KUHHHK
GUHH.
POOR SUPER SUPER POTATO!
NUMBER THREE! NUMBER FOUR!
SUPER POTATO IS ABOUT TO PASS OUT!
GET READY TO PICK HIM UP!
MINI-SHIP FOR THE MINI-MALICIAS.
HIGH-SECURITY POTATO CHAMBER.
RIGHT AWAY!
HOLD IT!!

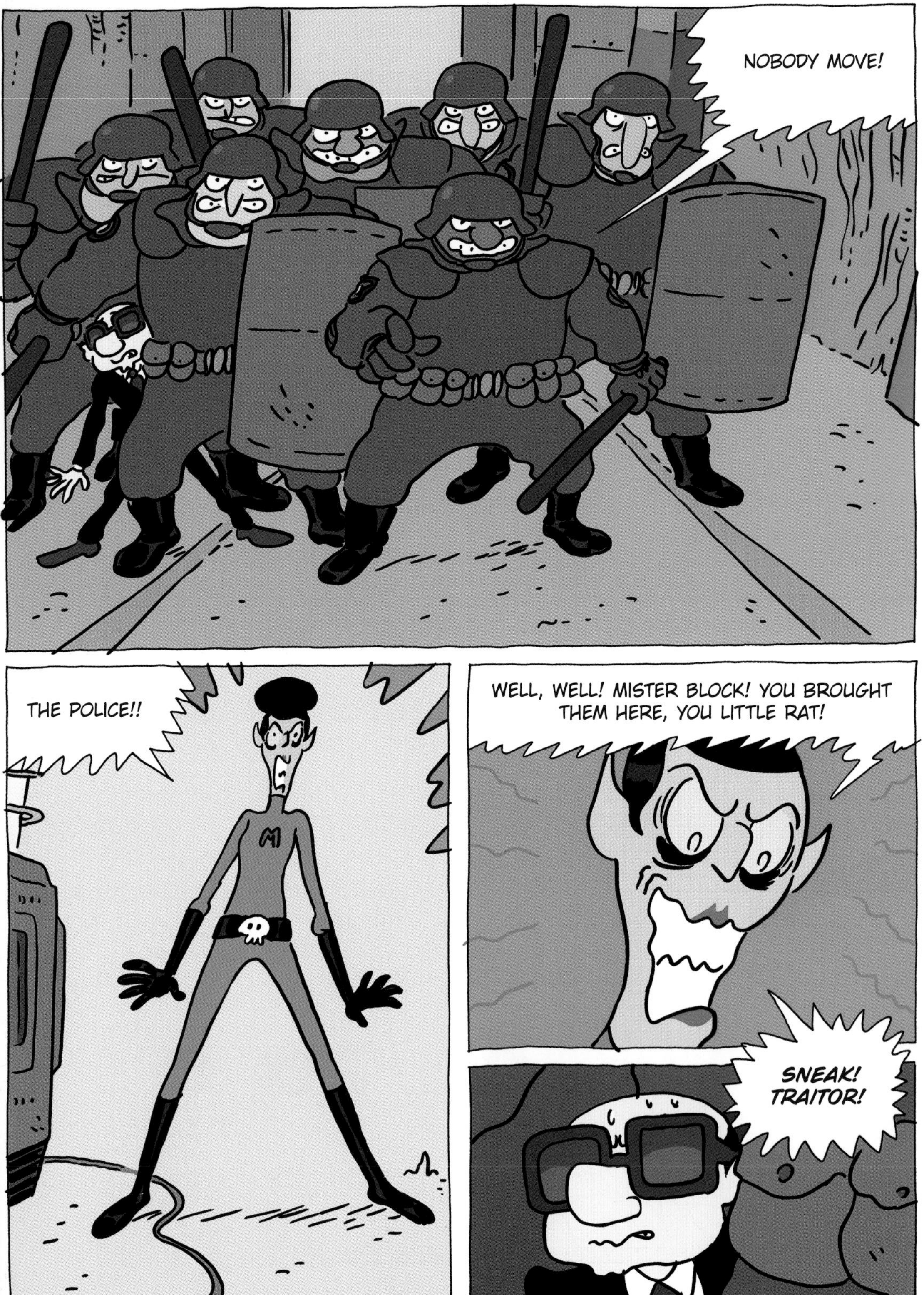
NOBODY MOVE!
THE POLICE!!
WELL, WELL! MISTER BLOCK! YOU BROUGHT THEM HERE, YOU LITTLE RAT!
SNEAK! TRAITOR!

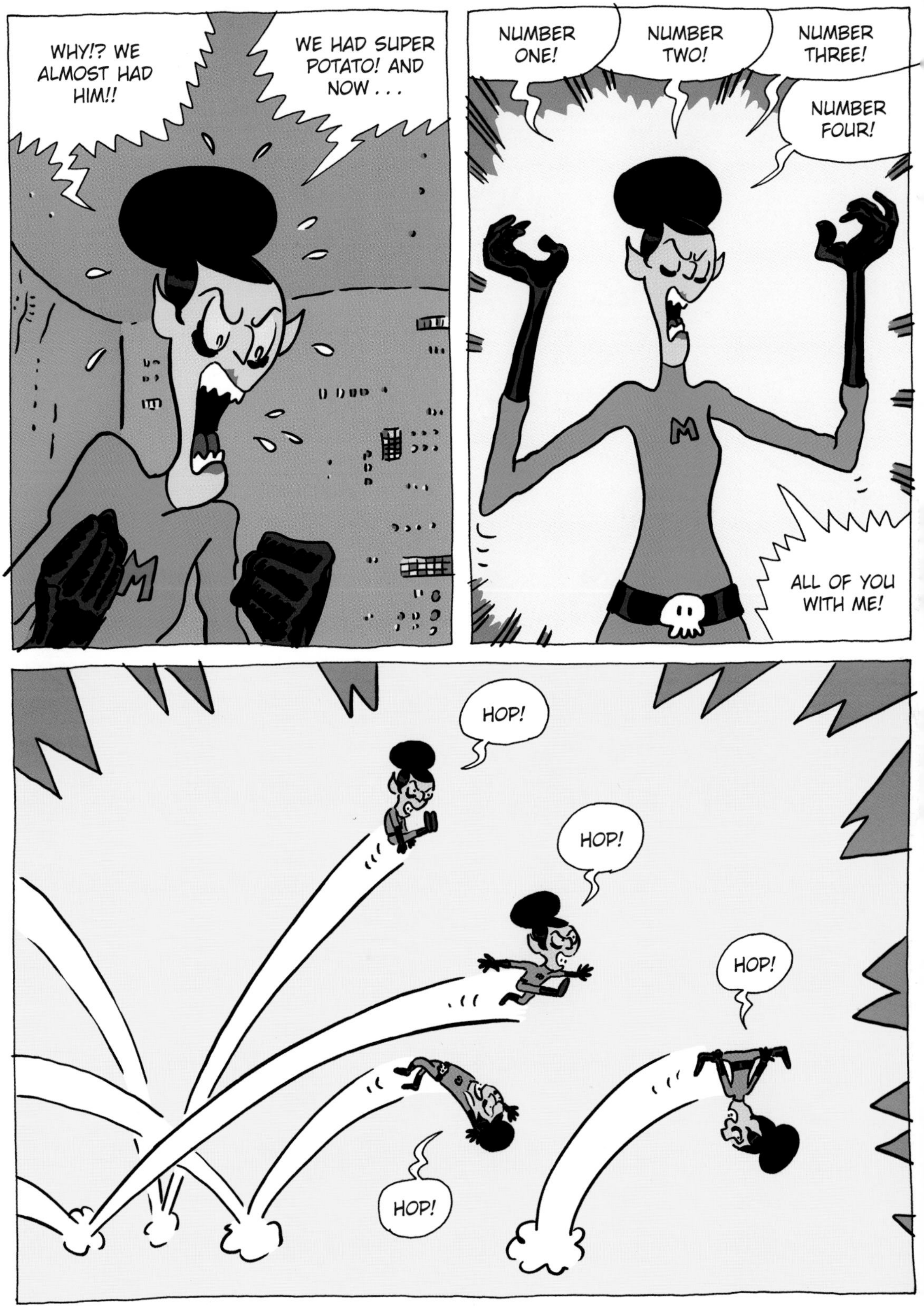
WHY!? WE ALMOST HAD HIM!!
WE HAD SUPER POTATO! AND NOW . . .
NUMBER ONE!
NUMBER TWO!
NUMBER THREE!
NUMBER FOUR!
ALL OF YOU WITH ME!
HOP!
HOP!
HOP!
HOP!

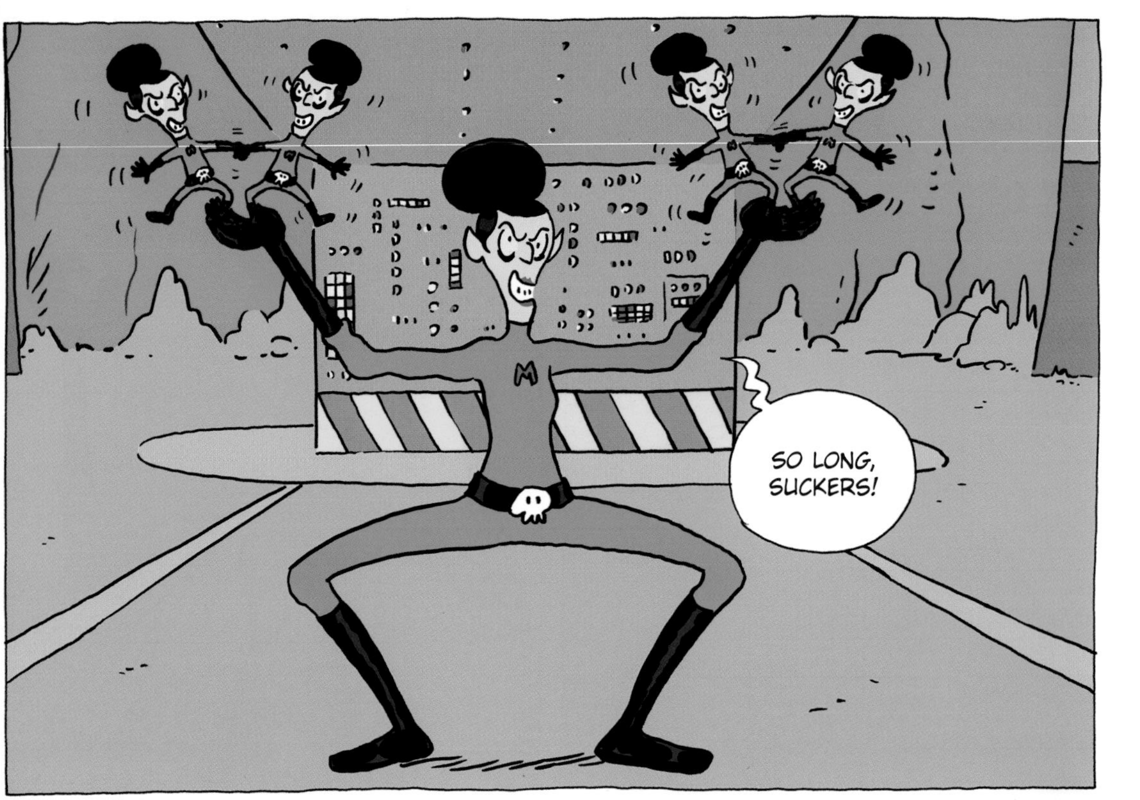
SO LONG, SUCKERS!

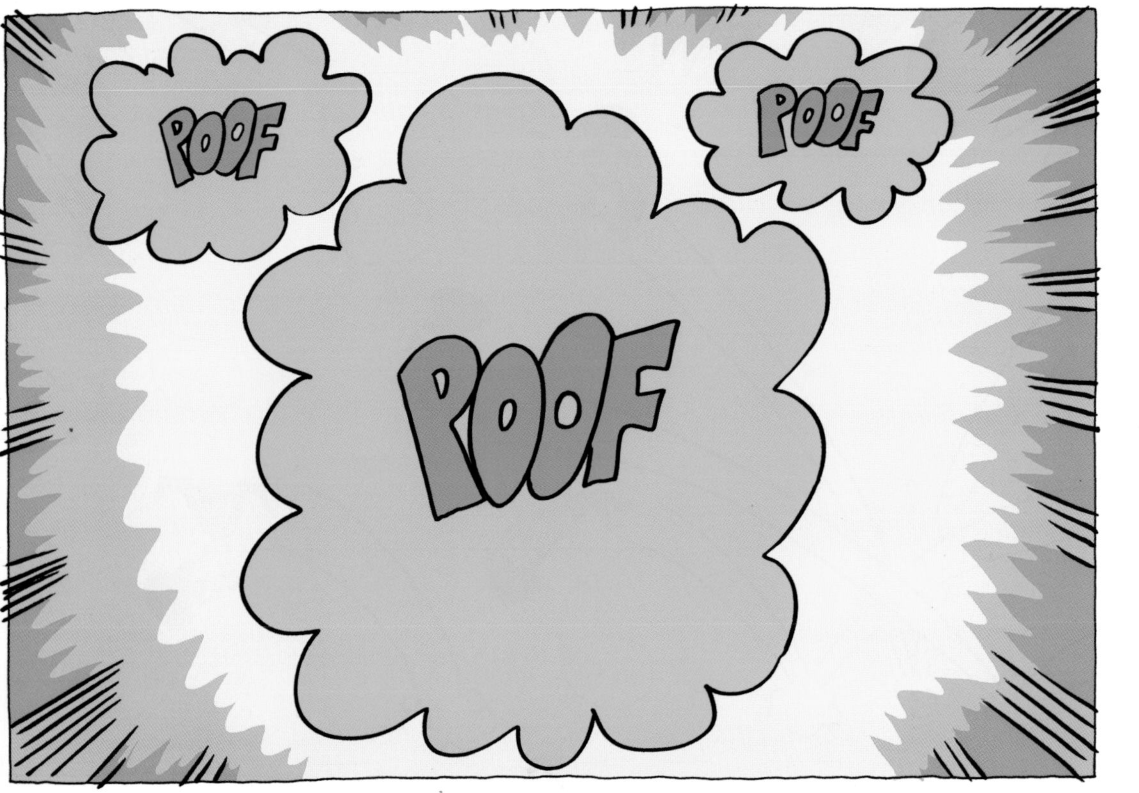
POOF
POOF
POOF

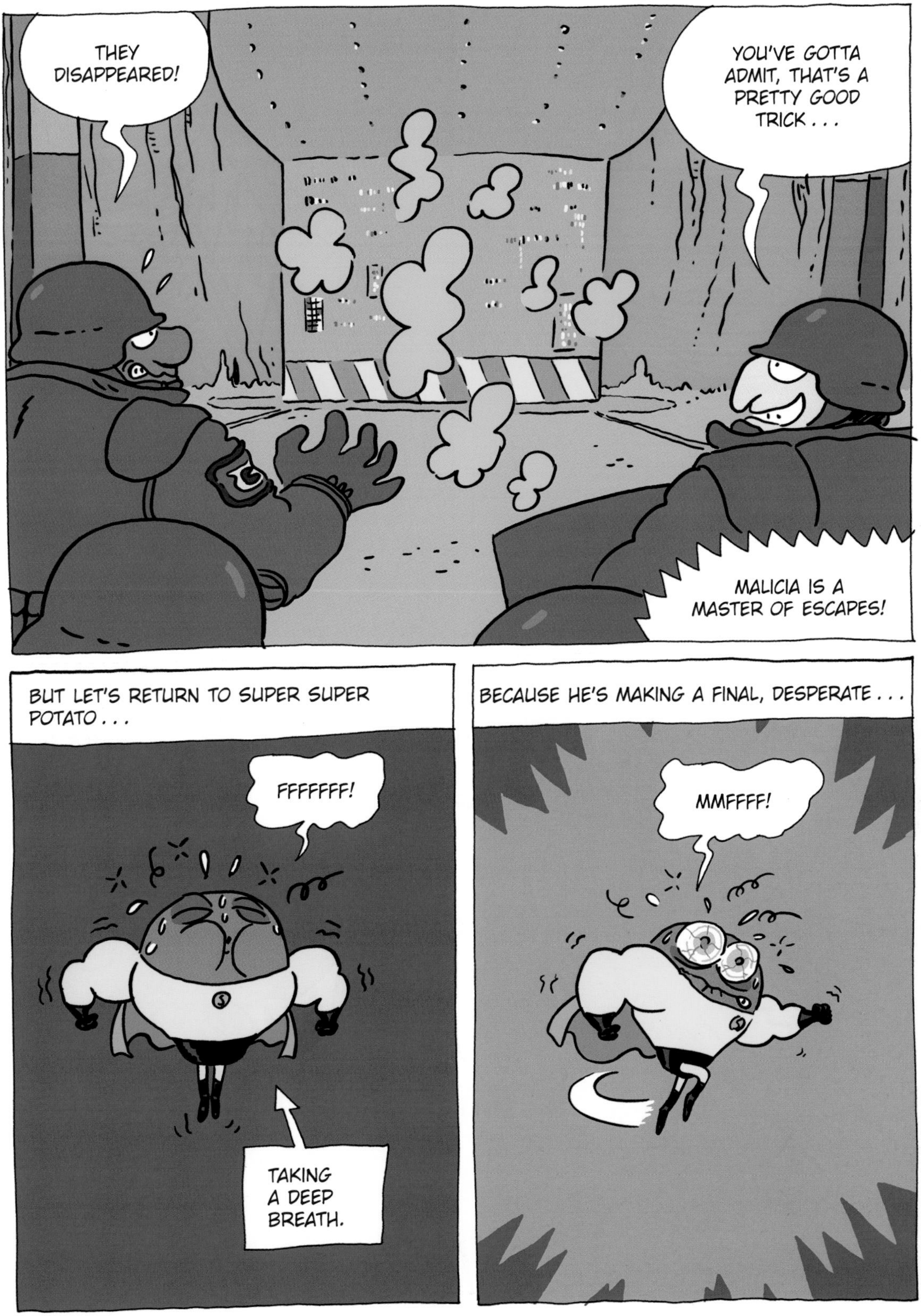
THEY DISAPPEARED!
YOU'VE GOTTA ADMIT, THAT'S A PRETTY GOOD TRICK . . .
MALICIA IS A MASTER OF ESCAPES!
BUT LET'S RETURN TO SUPER SUPER POTATO . . .
FFFFFFF!
TAKING A DEEP BREATH.
BECAUSE HE'S MAKING A FINAL, DESPERATE . . .
MMFFFF!

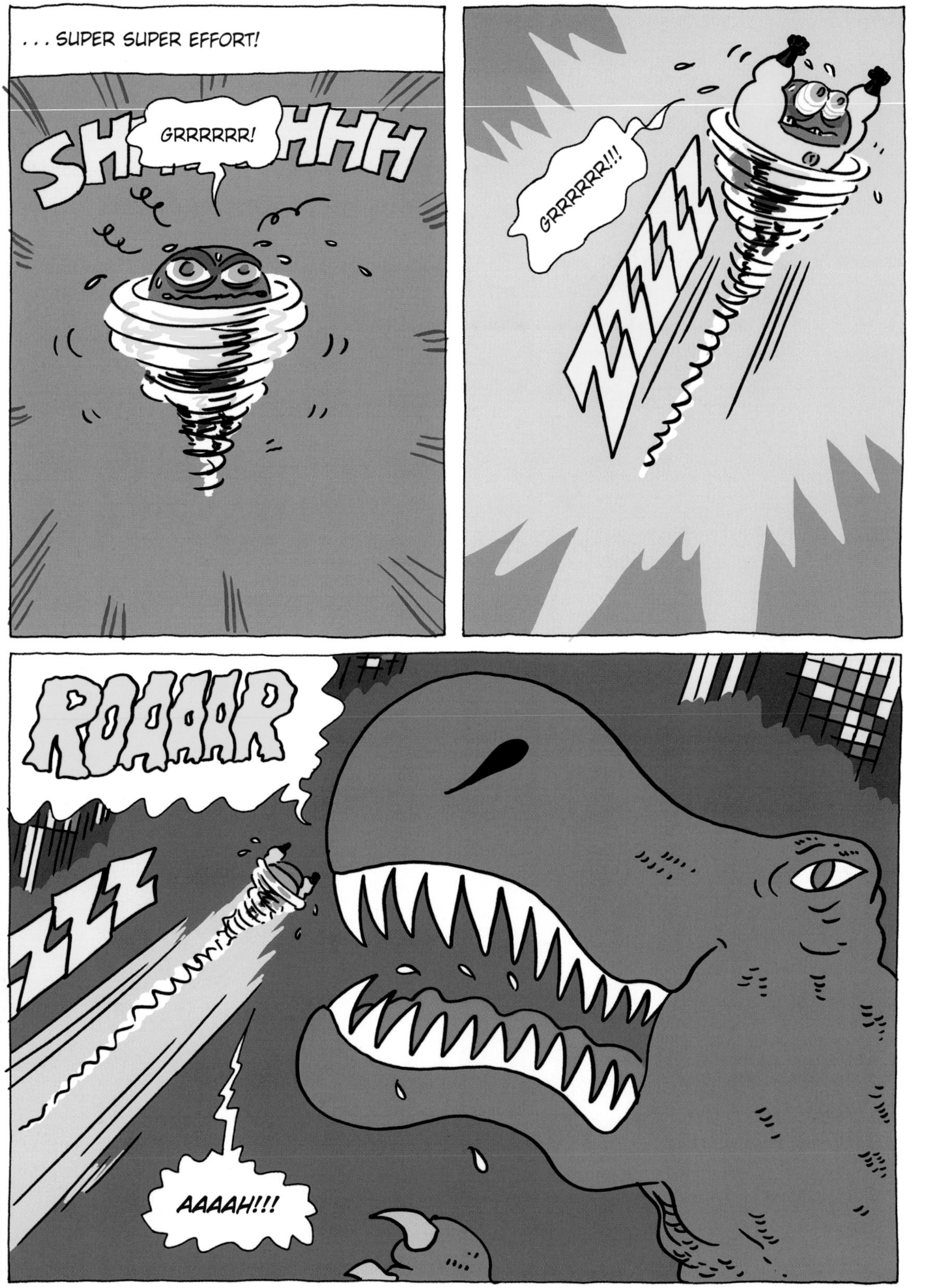
. . . SUPER SUPER EFFORT!
SHHHHHH
GRRRRRR!
GRRRRRR!!!
ZZZZ
ROAAAR
ZZZ
AAAAH!!!

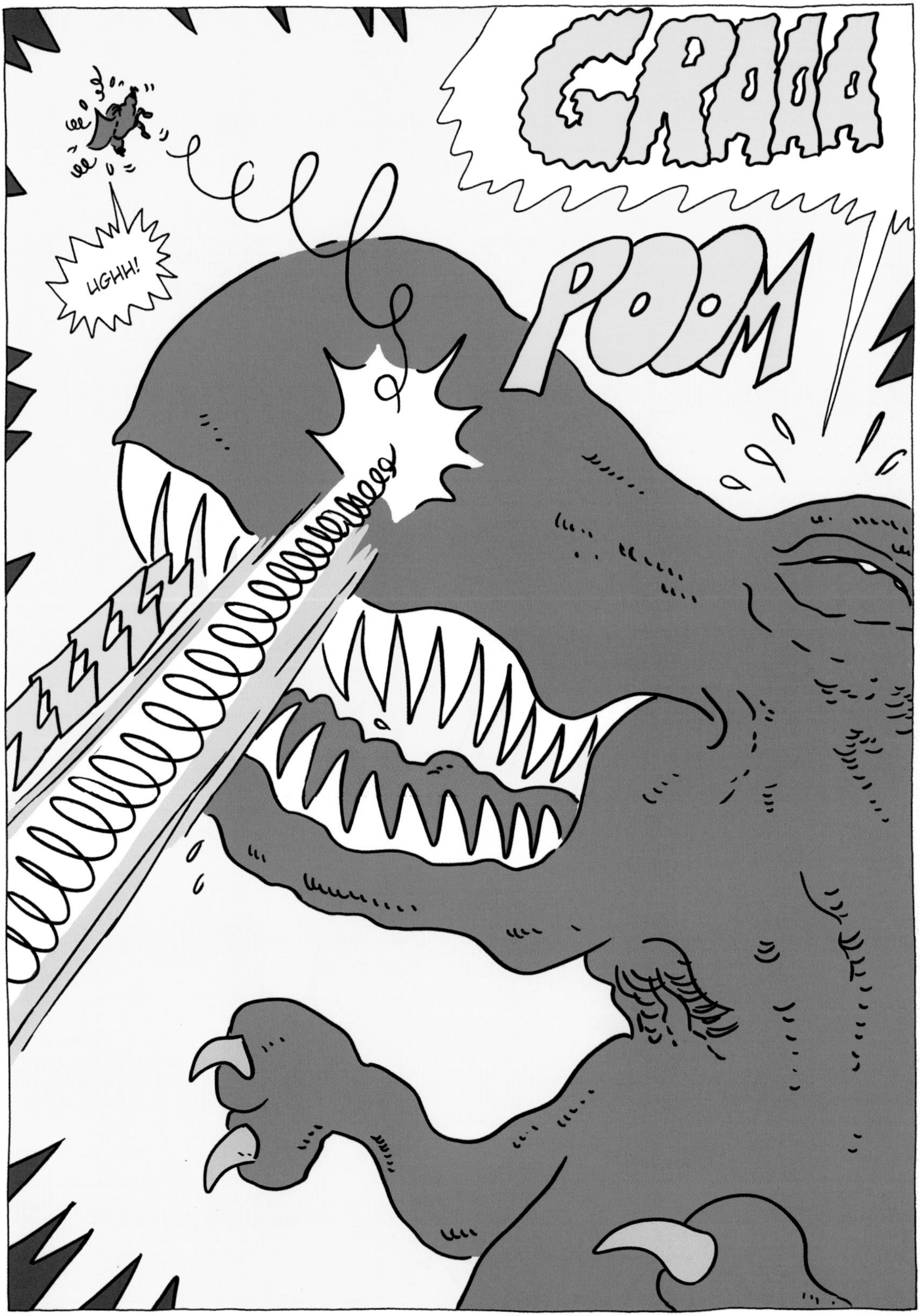
UGHH!
GRAAA
POOM

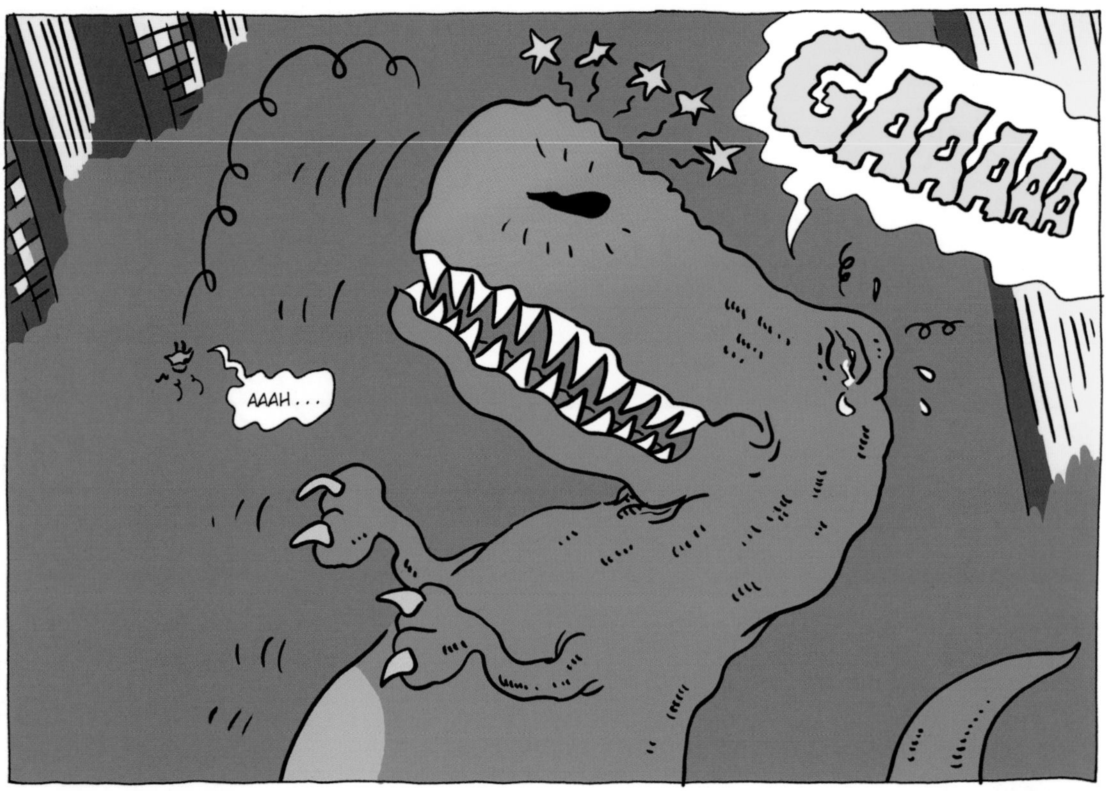
AAAH...
GAAAAA

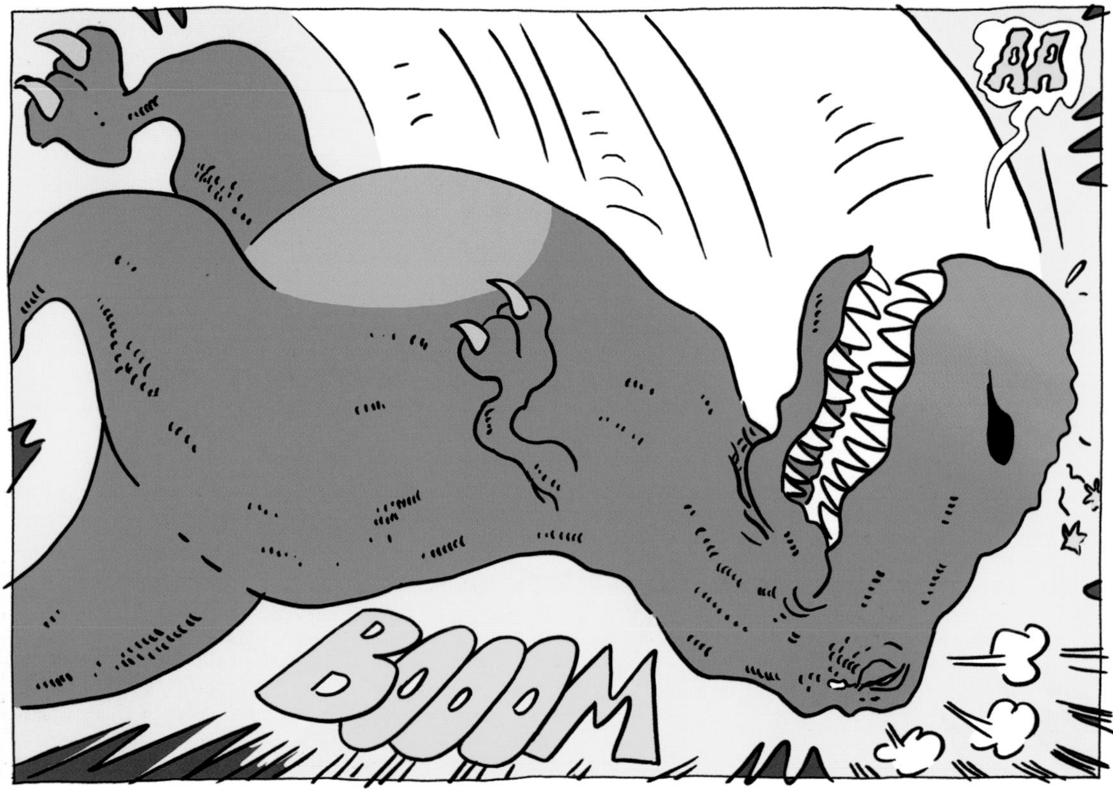
AA
BOOOM

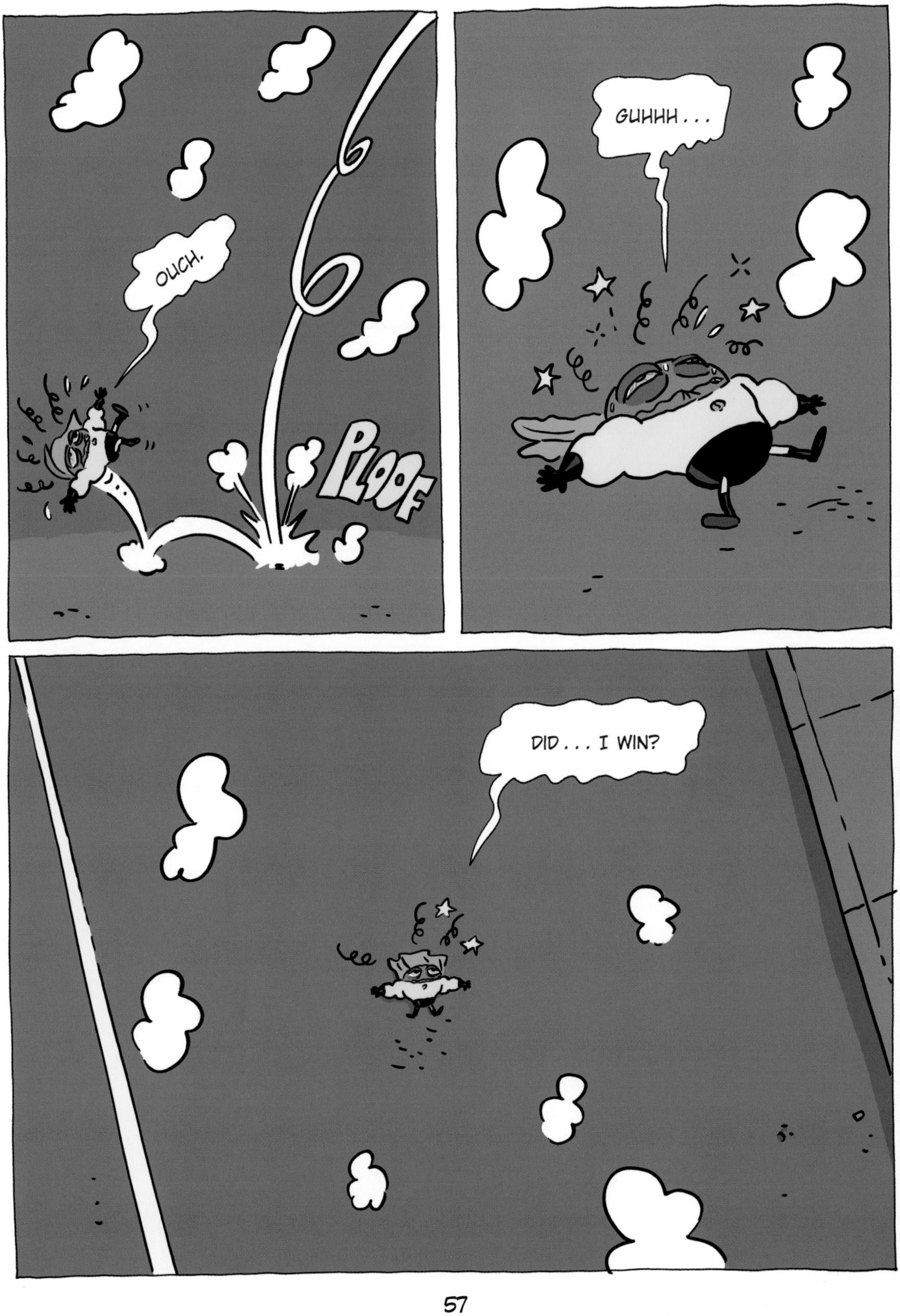
OUCH.
PLOOF
GUHHH . . .
DID . . . I WIN?

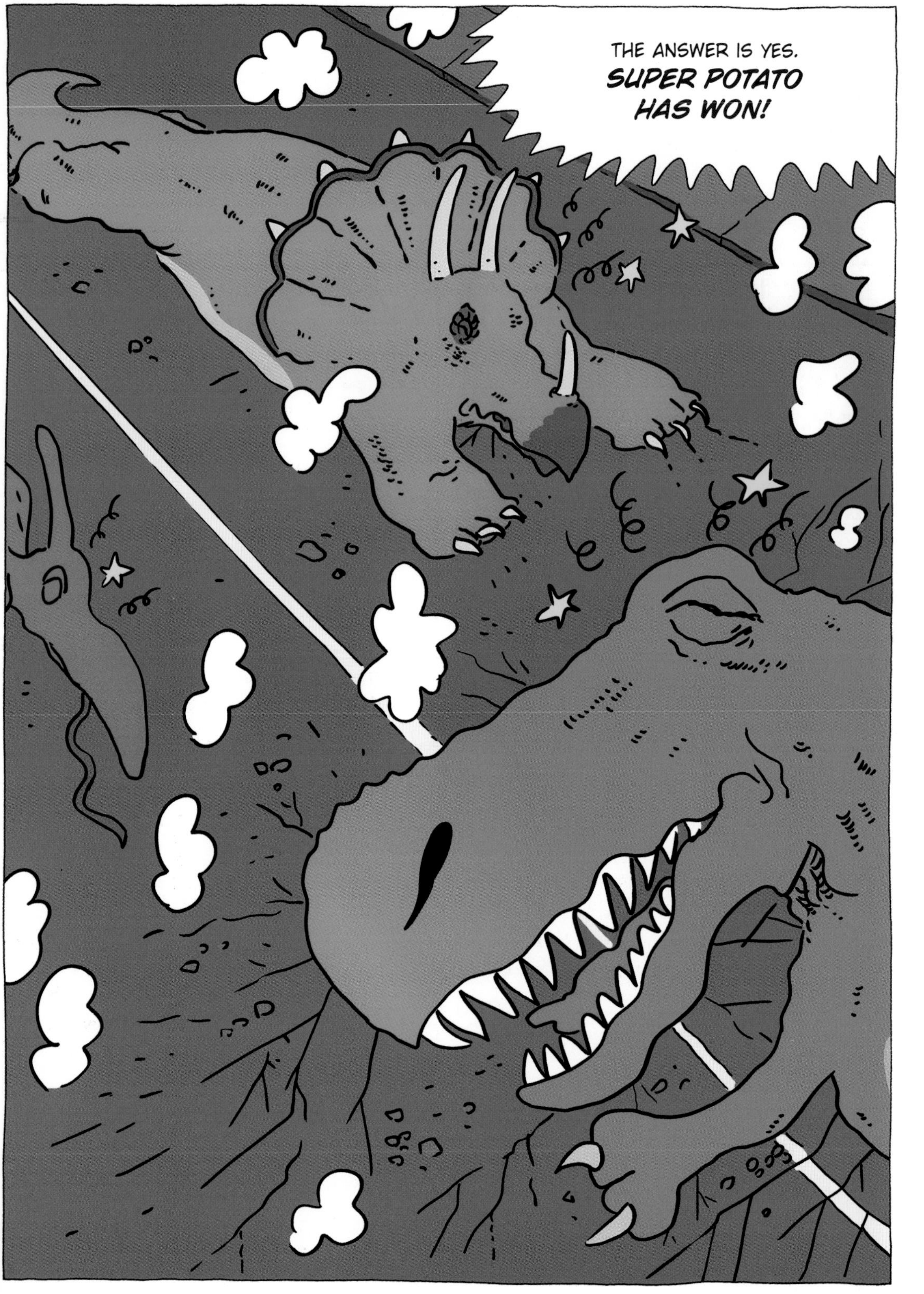
THE ANSWER IS YES.
SUPER POTATO HAS WON!

AT FIRST, THE AUTHORITIES PLACE THE PTEROSAURS IN THE BIRD SANCTUARY OF A LOCAL BOTANICAL GARDEN . . .

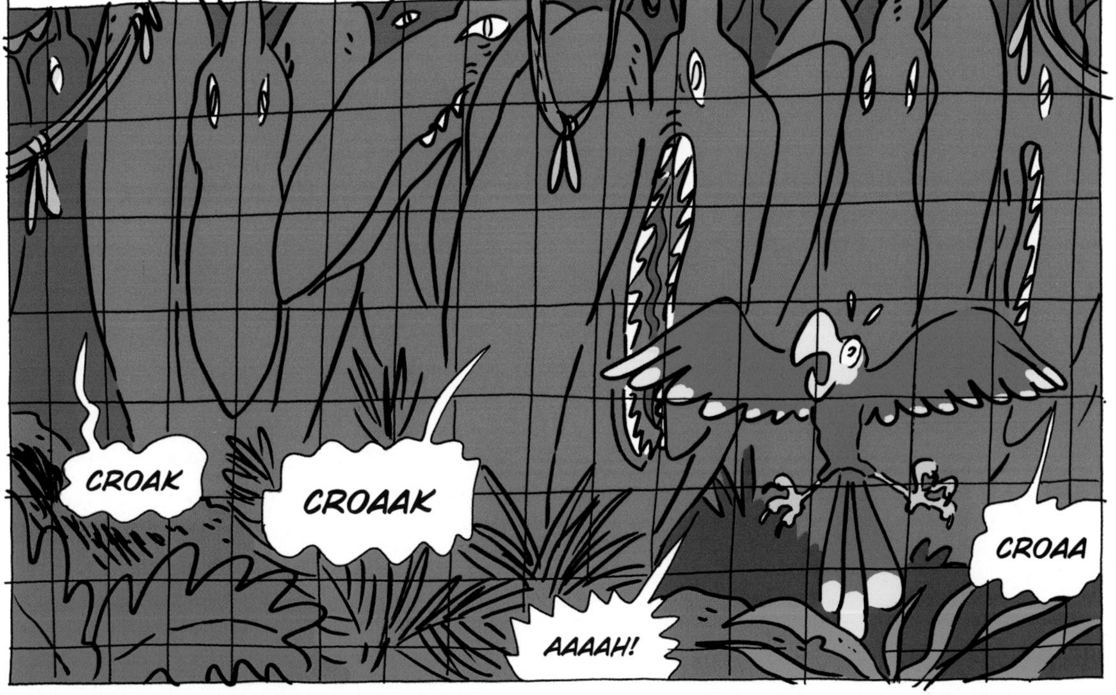

CROAK
CROAAK
CROAA
AAAAH!

. . . AND THE TRICERATOPSES AND THE T-REX IN THE CROCODILE TERRARIUM OF THE NATURAL HISTORY MUSEUM.

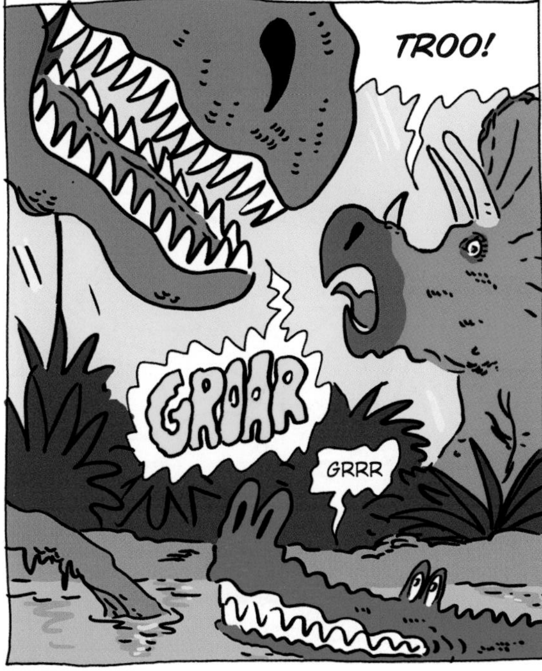

TROO!
GROAR
GRRR

LATER, THEY SEND THE CREATURES TO AN ISLAND WHERE THEY CAN ROAR ALL THEY WANT.

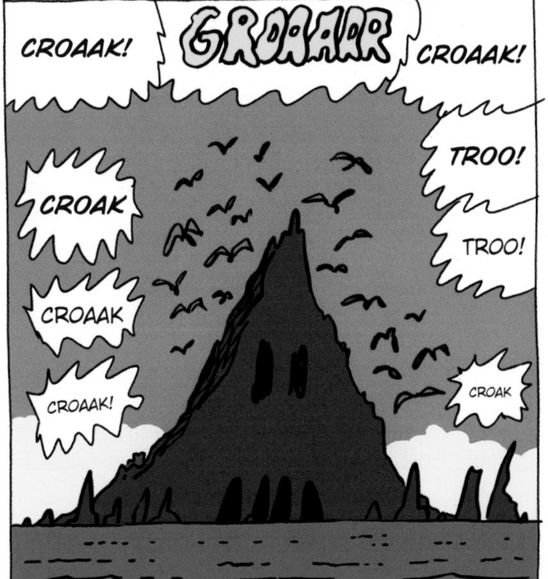

CROAAK!
GROAAAR
CROAAK!
TROO!
CROAK
TROO!
CROAAK
CROAAK!
CROAK

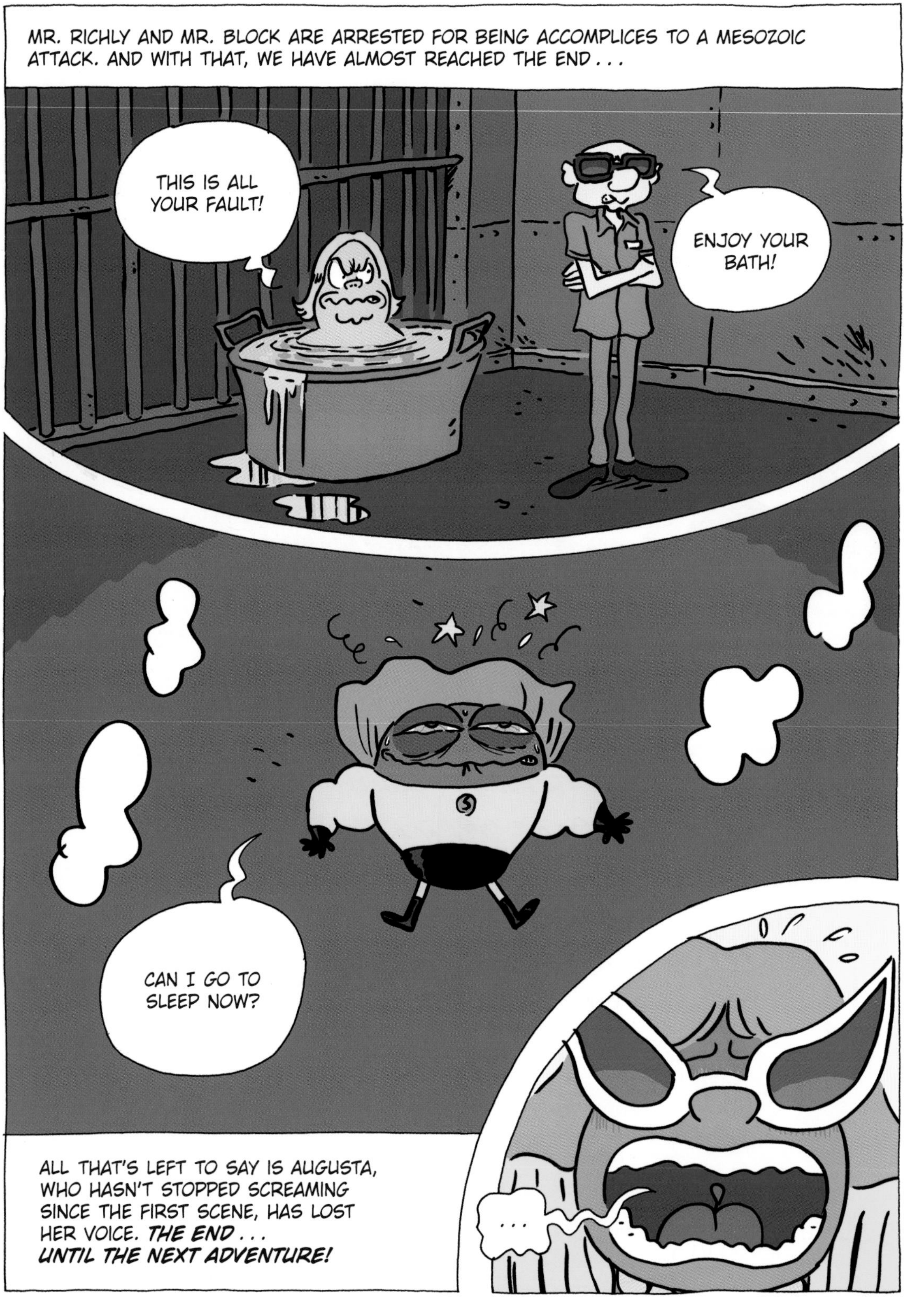
MR. RICHLY AND MR. BLOCK ARE ARRESTED FOR BEING ACCOMPLICES TO A MESOZOIC ATTACK. AND WITH THAT, WE HAVE ALMOST REACHED THE END . . .
THIS IS ALL YOUR FAULT!
ENJOY YOUR BATH!
CAN I GO TO SLEEP NOW?
ALL THAT'S LEFT TO SAY IS AUGUSTA, WHO HASN'T STOPPED SCREAMING SINCE THE FIRST SCENE, HAS LOST HER VOICE. ***THE END . . .***
UNTIL THE NEXT ADVENTURE!
. . .

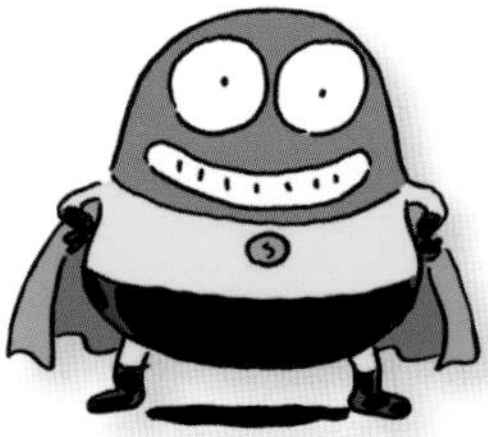

For more hilarious tales of Super Potato, check out . . .

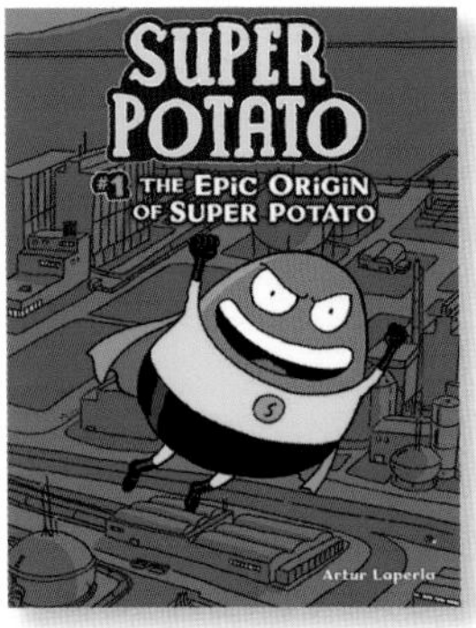
SUPER POTATO
#1 THE EPIC ORIGIN OF SUPER POTATO
Artur Laperla

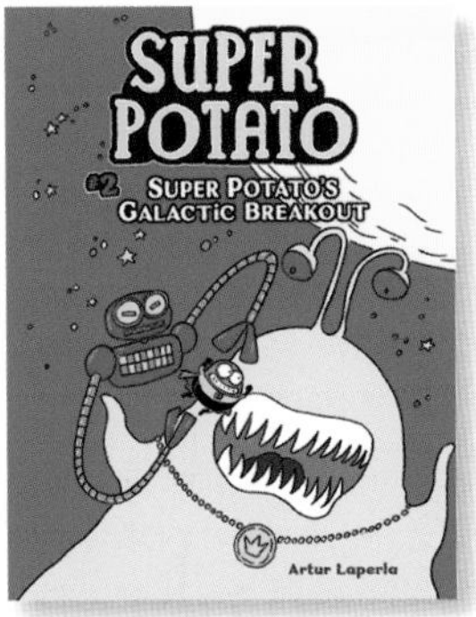
SUPER POTATO
#2 SUPER POTATO'S GALACTIC BREAKOUT
Artur Laperla

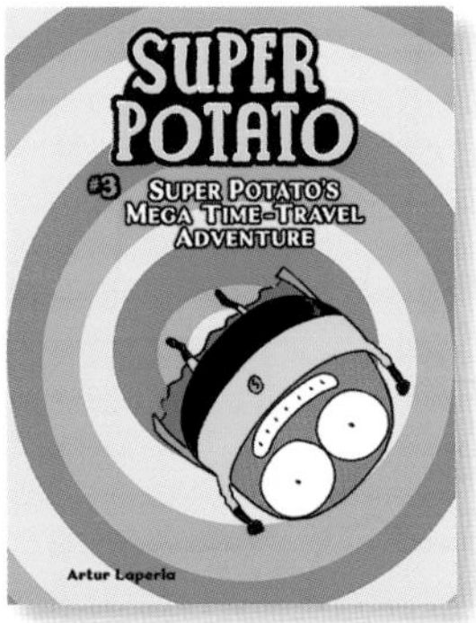
SUPER POTATO
#3 SUPER POTATO'S MEGA TIME-TRAVEL ADVENTURE
Artur Laperla

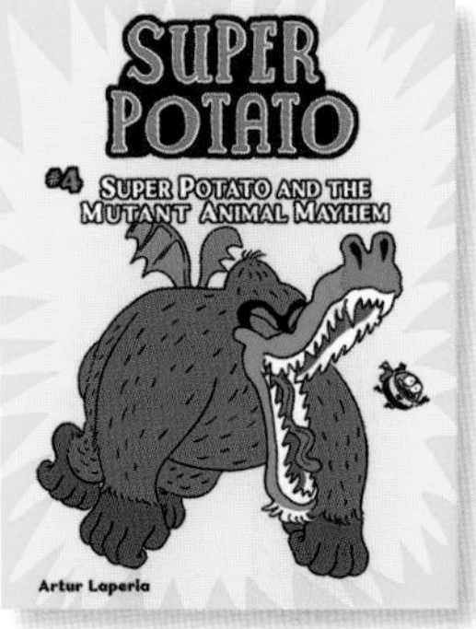
SUPER POTATO
#4 SUPER POTATO AND THE MUTANT ANIMAL MAYHEM
Artur Laperla

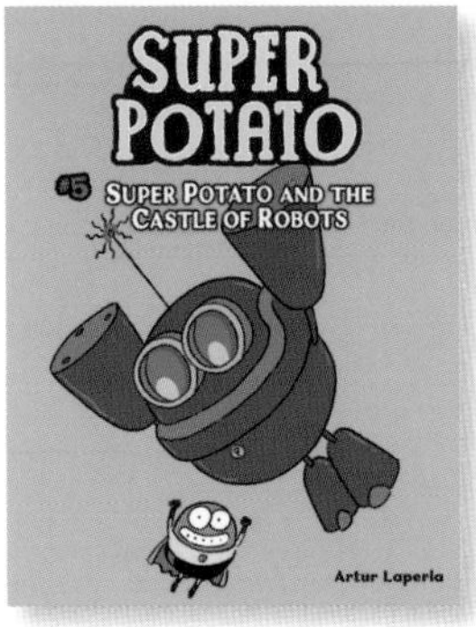
SUPER POTATO
#5 SUPER POTATO AND THE CASTLE OF ROBOTS
Artur Laperla

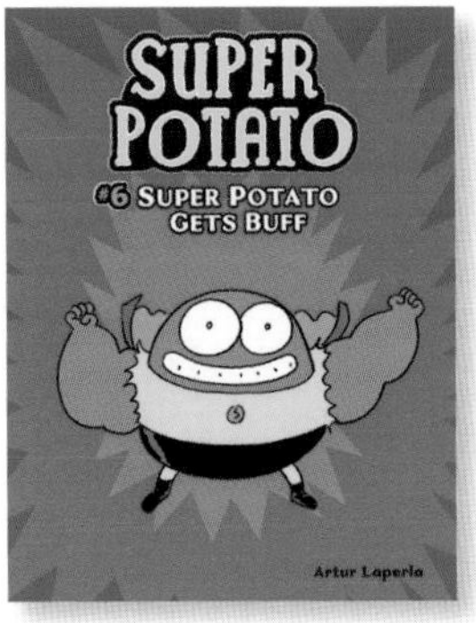
SUPER POTATO
#6 SUPER POTATO GETS BUFF
Artur Laperla

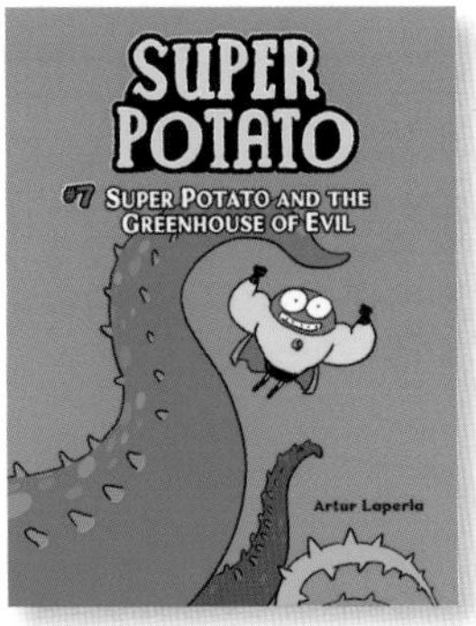
SUPER POTATO
#7 SUPER POTATO AND THE GREENHOUSE OF EVIL
Artur Laperla

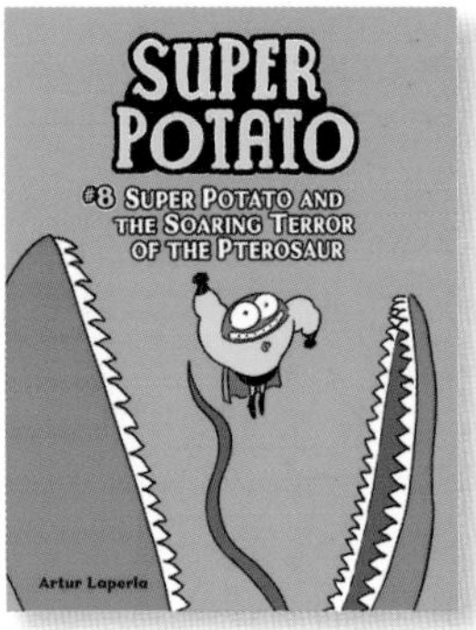
SUPER POTATO
#8 SUPER POTATO AND THE SOARING TERROR OF THE PTEROSAUR
Artur Laperla

AND TURN THE PAGE FOR A PREVIEW OF OUR HERO'S NEXT ADVENTURE . . .

SUPER POTATO #10

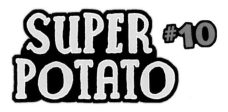

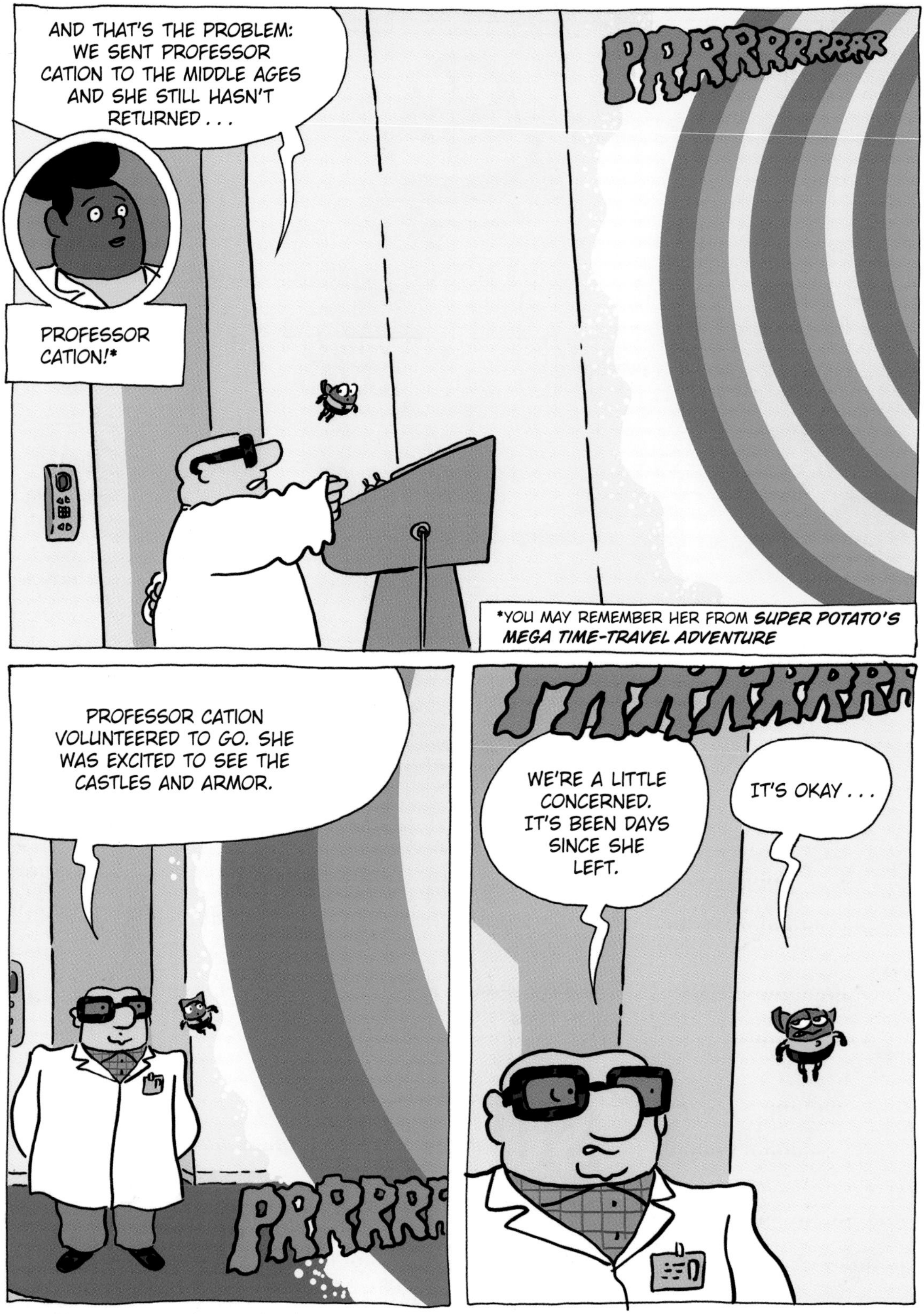
AND THAT'S THE PROBLEM: WE SENT PROFESSOR CATION TO THE MIDDLE AGES AND SHE STILL HASN'T RETURNED . . .
PRRRRRRRRR
PROFESSOR CATION!*
*YOU MAY REMEMBER HER FROM SUPER POTATO'S MEGA TIME-TRAVEL ADVENTURE
PROFESSOR CATION VOLUNTEERED TO GO. SHE WAS EXCITED TO SEE THE CASTLES AND ARMOR.
PRRRRR
WE'RE A LITTLE CONCERNED. IT'S BEEN DAYS SINCE SHE LEFT.
IT'S OKAY . . .

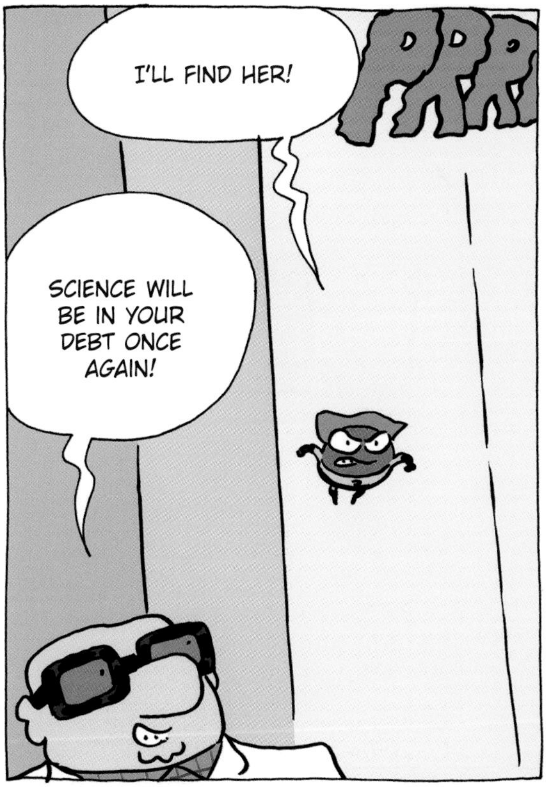
I'LL FIND HER!
SCIENCE WILL BE IN YOUR DEBT ONCE AGAIN!

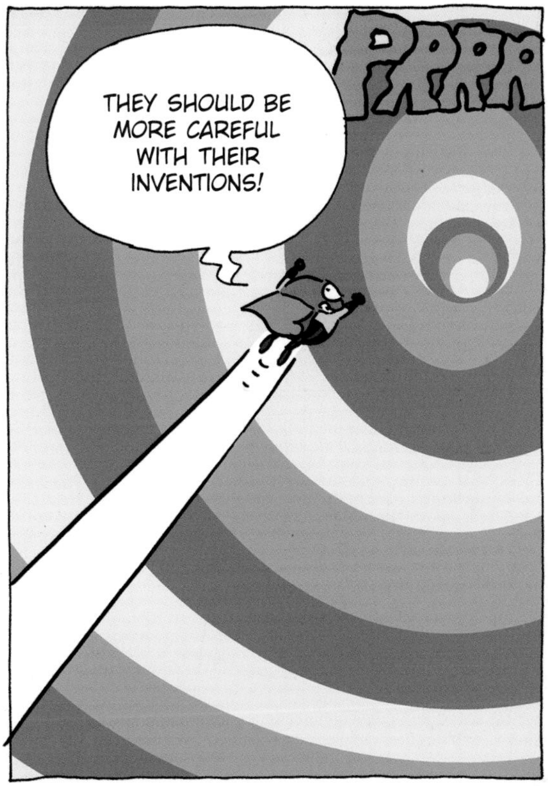
THEY SHOULD BE MORE CAREFUL WITH THEIR INVENTIONS!

SUPER POTATO GOES THROUGH THE PORTAL AND BEGINS TRAVELING TOWARD THE MIDDLE AGES!

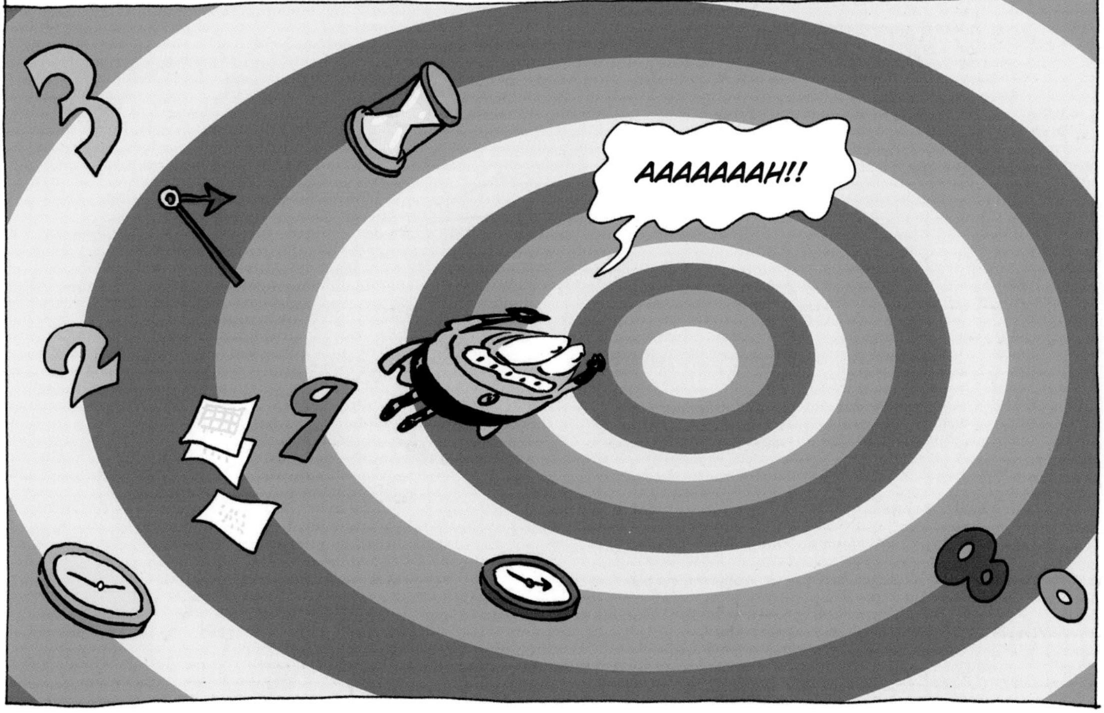
AAAAAAAH!!

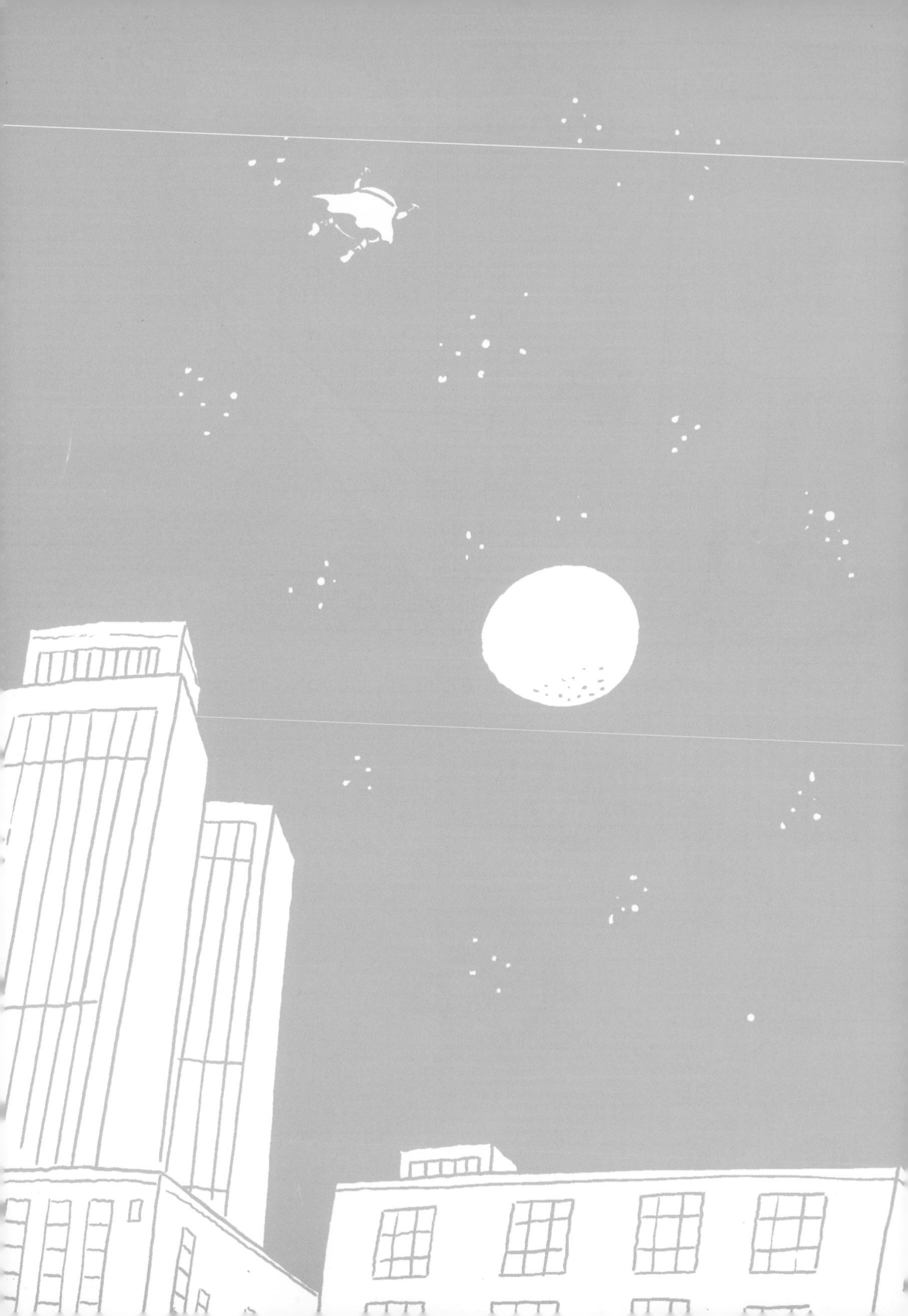